BOOMER BABES

*True Tales of Love
and Lust in the Later Years*

BOOMER BABES

*True Tales of Love
and Lust in the Later Years*

MARIA GRAZIA SWAN

LEISURE BOOKS NEW YORK CITY

A LEISURE BOOK®

May 2008

Published by

Dorchester Publishing Co., Inc.
200 Madison Avenue
New York, NY 10016

ISBN 10: 0-8439-5971-1
ISBN 13: 978-0-8439-5971-0

Visit us on the web at www.dorchesterpub.com.

In Memory

Alice D, Claudia L, Cathy S, Yvonne, Maria Teresa.

ACKNOWLEDGMENTS

To Jay Poynor, my agent, and Leah Hultenschmidt, editor extraordinaire, for believing in my book.

To Patricia Turpin for reminding me how to "punch up" my voice and to Lauren Hidden for making sure it was grammatically correct.

To Kathy Evenson-Howard, the captivating creator and leader of Body Buddies, the group that gave me my first glimpse into the fascinating world of Boomer Babes.

Special thanks to you, the reader, for picking up the book. May all your dreams of love and lust become reality. AMEN!

Contents

Introduction

I get out a lot, and I've got the stories to show for it. The other day I heard a woman declare that baby boomers invented love. Whoa, that's a big load to carry around, *inventors of love*. So what filled human hearts before the boomers came along? Surely love existed, maybe under a different name or maybe undercover. *Undercover,* yes, that must be where baby boomers found love, under the covers.

Even if boomers did not invent love, they did bring the art of loving to a new level. Can you think of any other generation that openly acknowledged—no, let me rephrase that, openly *embraced*—sex over fifty? And over sixty? And I bet the seventies don't stop us either. Nothing will stop boomers from loving, save the Grim Reaper, and some of my friends would even hit on him.

But while on the surface all appears well and drama free, the path to this long-brewing sexual freedom is the result of careful planning, intelligent budgeting, risk taking, and incredible self-love. Gone is the hush-hush of our parents' bedroom etiquette; today's lovers are open and almost flaunting of their sexual activities. And they look good doing it! I offer this book as a form of recognition—no, as a celebration—of the new sense of joy boomers have brought into the love lives of everyone over forty. My goal is to write something that inspires boomers to think young, act young, and embrace sexuality at any stage of life.

For each baby boomer in a happy, fulfilling relationship, there are at least three still looking, or looking again, for love. Although they don't seen to be looking very hard, and in my opinion, they aren't *really* looking at all. It's not a conscious decision; our daily routines simply don't facilitate romantic liaisons. We make choices designed to make our lives faster and, usually, less interactive. We drive more, walk less. We cyber talk instead of visiting in person. We shop online to avoid crowded malls. We use drive-throughs while talking on our cell phones. Most of the time we are totally oblivious of our surroundings and to the people around us. And to top it off, even if we do notice someone interesting, we're so bombarded with warnings of "stranger danger" that we don't dare approach him or her. Our resistance to actual face-to-face intermingling is so high that we even date online. Yes, we are introduced, date, and break up without ever having actually met the object of our desire.

Maybe that's a positive thing. The fantasy can remain unspoiled. I'm as guilty as anyone else of playing the game to my advantage. Shave a few years off the birthday, use a photo from younger times, spice up details of the daily routine to make life sound more interesting. By the time we're done embellishing our resumes, we sound so desirable we almost fall in love with ourselves. No surprise that when the time arrives to actually meet our potential mate face-to-face, we lock the doors, unplug the phone and computer, and hunker down in our bedroom like a kid in time-out.

On that note, I like to compare the routine of our daily lives to bricks that we stack around us. While we stack with security in mind, we create walls that keep the rest of the world out. We feel safe inside our self-built castle, safe and lonely. Then one day we ask ourselves: "Is this all there is?" We may become depressed, eat more chocolate, drink another glass of wine, acquire one more fluffy cat or curly-haired dog, add more channels to our cable service, read the latest book on relationships, sign up for one more Internet dating site, and generally make our fortress stronger.

That's part of the reason matchmaking businesses are sprouting up and growing by leaps and bounds. I had an interesting conversation with the CEO of one such enterprise. We discussed—what else?—single baby boomers. She said that any man over fifty who is single, self-supporting, and in good health should be offered compensation, as opposed to paying a fee, for the privilege of being entered in a matchmaking database. That tells you how scarce single male boomers are. Scarce, but not extinct. Don't take this statement as a sign of surrender. Men are out there. They aren't hiding or playing hard to get. They are as much victims of modern circumstances as their female counterparts.

But there is a whole rebellious movement out there. After all, these are the same women who fostered and embraced Women's Lib. They did a lot more than burn their bras; they fought stereotyped images of how women should live, work, marry, remarry, and reproduce. Today's baby boomers are realizing their inner strengths, their hidden powers. Women are hitting on men, often younger men. Men are getting face-lifts, hair transplants, and buying skin moisturizers! It is a generational revolution, and there is strength in numbers.

In this very decade, there will be more people over sixty-five in the United States than people under twenty. All we need is a little push, some encouragement, and we can all work toward enriching our daily lives with love. Okay, maybe you are more interested in sex than love, or maybe to you they are one and the same. Whatever your interest, I'm hoping that you'll recognize yourself in one of my stories and perhaps be inspired to seek new romantic ventures by the others.

Because I am single and female, most of my stories come from my female friends, single, quasi-single, or single-minded. As time goes by, it becomes more evident that in the case of boomers, age really is a state of mind. They enjoy more sex, with more partners, without making a big deal out of it. Love and sex, not necessarily in that order, are a vital part of their lives. Since the love lives of my baby boomer friends are instructive, often hilarious, and occasionally titillating, I just couldn't live with myself if I didn't share them with the world.

Names have been changed to protect the innocent . . . and the *totally* guilty.

The Trailblazers

The Trailblazers

"There is nothing half so real in life as the things you've done . . . inexorably, unalterably done."—**Sara Teasdale**

No, I'm not talking about the roaring *zoom, zoom, zoom* of motorcycle racing, or the off-road exploits of four-wheel-drive trucks, and none of these trailblazers bites the dust. Okay, maybe some do, but only the bad guys. These trailblazers are ordinary people, coping as best as possible, but when unforeseen circumstances arise, instead of running or hiding, they respond with genuine creativity. What sets these people apart is the way they act or react to life events and go on to create a win–win experience for everyone involved. Okay, almost everyone. Have no idea what I'm talking about? Would you like an example of an ordinary person, unforeseen circumstances, and an astonishing outcome? The story I'm about to tell you was related to me by a professor when I was living in France.

This is about an artist. A female artist whose name I can't remember. Let's call her Colette. Young Colette was a painter; she painted with oil. This is beginning to sound like the introduction to a bad movie, but stick with me, it gets better. The professor never said where Colette's studio was, but I picture her in a tiny room, up high in a sunny attic somewhere in Montmartre; I smell paint thinner in the air, and see floating blond hair a la Deneuve; she has a Mona Lisa smile on her pretty face. This young artist had a lover, like all French women apparently do, and on this particular day they were to meet for "lunch." Colette went to put her paintbrushes in the jar filled with acetone before leaving for her rendezvous. In her rush to see her lover, she bumped against the jar, and it tipped over spilling acetone on the table and everything on it. One of the things on the table was a small pink hair comb. Since this happened a long time ago, before the discovery of plastic, Colette's small pink hair comb was made of celluloid. When celluloid comes in contact with acetone, it melts. Our artist-who-looked-like-Deneuve tried to contain the mess and while doing so, got some melted celluloid on her fingernails. She stopped and admired the bright pink spots on her nails and being a saucy little thing, left the pink in place and went to lunch. And there you have it, the discovery of modern-day nail polish. Is this story true or a myth? I'm not sure, but it is a nice tale, and it helps to make my point: Seeming disasters can lead to new fun discoveries if you have an open mind.

Want to know if you have what it takes to be a trailblazer? Take this quick quiz to find out.

Trailblazers 101

A Quiz

1. It's your day off and it's pouring rain. You:

    a. Decide to stay home cleaning your closets—after all, it's a wasted day.

    b. Grab your poncho and go splish-splashing through the streets to get done what you need to do that day.

    c. Call your close friends and organize an impromptu skinny-dipping party in the backyard pool. Hey, if rain is good for plants, it must be good for your skin and hair, too.

2. You're in your car, waiting for the traffic light to change when you notice that a young mother and child just missed the bus. You:

    a. Flash them a sympathetic smile and drive away when the light changes.

   b. Roll down the car window and assure them the next bus will be around soon.

   c. Offer the young mom and the child a ride.

3. Your significant other announced, for the hundredth time, that you would be perfect if only you'd lose fifteen pounds. He promises you $5,000 toward a new car if you lose the weight. You:

   a. Tell him the best way to lose some extra weight is to get rid of him, storm out the door, and vow never to go back.

   b. Lose the weight, cash the check, and tell him he is no longer significant.

   c. Join a swanky gym with an advance on the $5,000. You use the rest to buy new clothing with a slimming effect and start dating your personal trainer from the gym.

4. You go shopping with a girlfriend and you both fall in love with the same dress. The two of you wear the same size, and this is the last one available. You:

   a. Tell her it was your idea to go shopping; therefore you have first rights to buy it.

   b. Get into a catfight over the dress and accidentally rip it. You both quietly leave the store and go for ice cream.

   c. Since the dress fits you both you'll split the cost and co-own it. You decide to spend the savings on matching accessories.

5. Your co-workers are organizing a bridal shower for your boss, who gets married and divorced about twice a year. You:

   a. Think it's a pathetic waste of time and money so you decide to call in sick on the day of the shower.

b. Buy a very inexpensive gift and go to the shower to see what fool fell for your boss this time around.

c. Go with an open heart, an open mind, and a sterling silver photo frame. He can always replace the photo if he changes mates again.

6. Every time you show up for family gatherings you get picked on because everyone else is a couple. Thanksgiving is coming up and you are expected to make it home. You:

a. Are working on finding a good excuse not to go, even though it means so much to your family.

b. Are seriously considering borrowing a diamond ring from a friend and telling your family you're engaged to a foreigner whose flight was cancelled and therefore couldn't make it.

c. Called home and announced you were bringing guests. Then you invited Tom and Jeff, your good friends who are in a loving, committed relationship, and asked them to be your chaperones. You know you'll all have a good time and you three will be on your way back to the city before your family can figure out if this is a ménage à trois or something else.

7. Your best friend set you up for a blind date. She claims she knows you so well that this will be a perfect match. She has been wrong before, more than once. You know she means well. You:

a. Tell her thank you but no thank you.

b. Ask to check photos, dating history, financial background, even a dental chart—you're a stickler for good teeth—before committing to a meeting.

c. Decide it may be a total waste of time, but you never know—he could be your soul mate. You put on your favorite outfit, wear your lucky scarf, and show up at the appointed time with your brightest smile, linked arm-in-arm with your two single girlfriends who are dying to meet someone.

Are you trailblazer material?

If you have mostly C answers (five or more) you are a true trailblazer and you'll probably see yourself in some of the stories you are about to read.

On the other hand, if all your answers are A, you need to take a good look at what's going on here. Carpe diem, my friend. If there ever was a time to take chances, this is it—here, now, at this stage of life. Lighten up. I'm not suggesting you jump from a plane without a parachute. As a matter of fact, I'm not implying you jump from anything. Just be more open to new experiences. Mary McCarthy said it best: *We are the hero of our own story.* Be that hero.

If you answered B to more than five questions, you are trailblazer material, still rough around the edges. A little encouragement goes a long way. I bet after you read about the adventures of our trailblazers, you'll be ready to hit the discovery road at full speed.

Oh my! Your answers were the perfect mix of A, B, and C. You are totally in touch with yourself and can be whoever you want to be. All I can say here is: Good luck, enjoy the book, and have a happy, fulfilling love life.

Hair to Dye for: Lisa's Story

**Innovative solutions for graying hair. And we don't
mean the ones on your head.**

Boomer Babes is yet another boomer-gals group. Contrary
to the Blue Thong Society and the Red Hat Society, Boomer
Babes has no official chapters, no dues, no age requirements, and
no specific clothing to wear. They get together monthly at a
trendy establishment, and their main goals are to chat, eat, drink,
share information and sometimes gossip. In other words, they
like to have fun and do girl stuff.

Here's the scene: stylish Scottsdale, Arizona, in the fall, the
shaded patio of the "in" restaurant du jour; a group of picture-
perfect female boomers exchanging enlightening rumors and
tedious realities. No, this is not a scene from *Desperate Housewives
of the Southwest*; it is a monthly get-together, usually on Thurs-
days after yoga. We're all forty-something . . . plus something-
something. All single, either by marital status or state of mind. Lisa,
who is legally single, is telling us about her upcoming trip to Las
Vegas with Jeff.

Lisa and Jeff met at one of those electronics stores. She was
shopping for a gadget gift for her techie son, and, we assume,
Jeff noticed her look of bewilderment and came to her rescue.
She, however, insists he fell prey to her big blue eyes—twice
enhanced. Whatever the reason, he asked her out for drinks, one
thing led to another and now they've had several dates. Then
Lisa found out Jeff is married, but on the road to divorce.

Now his divorce is about to be finalized, and they're flying to
Vegas to celebrate. This will be their first time staying together
in close quarters for multiple nights, and Lisa is nervous. After

all, she explains, she feels crowded just sharing a bathroom, and she can't possibly suggest separate rooms, can she?

We, her wise and discerning Boomer Babe friends, aren't buying it.

"Lisa, what's really bugging you?" Kathy asks.

"Nothing." Lisa isn't a very good liar. "I'm not sure I want Jeff to see me without makeup."

"Say what?" That's from Sam, a serious outdoor lover who drives a stick shift and has been known to camp out alone. Her idea of makeup is tinted sunscreen and pink lip-gloss. "Hasn't he already seen you without makeup? Doesn't he spend the night at your house at least once a week?"

"Yes," says Lisa, "but I shower and remove my makeup, you know, *after*. In the morning, I get out of bed before him and make a beeline to the bathroom, where I put on my full makeup."

"Before coffee?" Sam is clearly shocked. I hush Sam; Lisa is bringing up some real issues here, and she isn't done yet.

"And then," she says, "there's the intimacy factor." She actually blushes. No one says a word. We know we're about to get a juicy tidbit out of her.

"I'll be, naked, and . . ."

"Excuse me," Sam again. The rest of us groan. Why must she get her two cents in now?

"You're concerned about being naked? What, have you two been having sex with your clothes on? Clothed, in the dark and with the curtains drawn, just in case? Do you put duct tape over the alarm clock for complete darkness?"

The rest of us feel sorry for Lisa; Sam is merciless. She once confessed that she eats at truck stops when she "needs her fix." Her none-too-delicate way of saying she's in the mood for sex. And Sam can stretch and twist on a yoga mat like the tail of a kite on a windy day. She's a truck driver's dream.

Feeling I need to come to the rescue, I say, "Lisa, you have a great body. You're full of energy. Jeff is a very lucky man."

"He is so young." Lisa sighs—and not the good kind of sigh

that means, *Yowza, so young, so beautiful, so strong*. No, this was the sad-sack sigh that means, *And I'm such a wrinkled old prune, it's just a matter of time until he sees me in good light and thinks "Omigod, have I been drunk for six months?"*

Now we are beginning to get to the real story. The same old story. Age difference.

"Maybe, but he looks older than you," I retort. And it's true. Jeff is one of those guys who, no matter what crowd he's in, looks like he must be someone's older uncle.

Lisa sighs again and runs rings around the rim of her glass with her well-manicured fingernail. "He has all his hair."

"So do you. At least, I think you do. That is your real hair on your head, isn't it? Not yours as in you paid for it? I mean, it's attached to your head genetically?" Sam is getting too personal, I think.

"It's my natural hair, but not the color."

"Big deal, so you color your hair. Most women our age do the same, more or less."

"It's the 'more' I'm wondering about," Lisa says, blushing again. She leans toward us. "Do they color just their head?" Her voice drops to a whisper. "Or do they color *all* their hair?"

It takes a moment to hit us: Lisa is concerned about her hair, not the ones on her head.

Sam is the first to break the pensive silence. "If he notices *that* color difference, he isn't, well, let's say in that case, he couldn't be fully engaged in loving your . . . *hairstyle* girl. Trust me on that one."

"I sometimes dye mine," states Michelle, a well-groomed Realtor, with a mix of pride and embarrassment, her chin slightly thrust out. There is a wave of recognition around the table. Of course she does! Michelle's nail color matches her lipstick. Her shoes are dyed to match her Ann Taylor suit. She never wears gold with silver. We suddenly realize her once-brunette eyebrows match her newly light auburn hair. Involuntarily, we all glance down at her lap. Then a multitude of questions.

"You do it yourself? What do you use?"

"Does it stain your skin? How do you keep it off the inside of your thighs?"

"Does it hurt? Do you have any allergic reaction down there?" The questions are popping like jumping beans in a Tijuana vendor's cart. We quiet down when we notice people at other tables staring at us.

"It's not a big deal," Michelle says, now slightly smug in her new role of worldly wise. "I only do it once in a while, for *special occasions*." She smiles. Yes, we got it.

Now that we're on the topic, ideas and questions flow. Roots touch up? Coloring shampoo? Salon professionals? Solitude? Sam exclaims, "Grecian Formula!" We all laugh. Kathy says she just plucks her gray ones with tweezers. Ouch.

Then Susan, the quiet one, drops the bomb: "Brazilian bikini wax." Conversation stops.

"You do that?" My voice is squeaky with imagined pain.

"Actually, no. But I have a friend who swears by it." What a relief! But she has our attention. We've all heard stories about the pain and the gain. We watched *Sex and the City*. But there is a lot we've watched Carrie Bradshaw and her friends do that we haven't, and won't try. Still, we want to know more: prices, duration, side effects. Susan promises us she will talk to her friend and get the skinny, so to speak.

Our lunch breaks up after that, because just what can you talk about after this kind of topic? A few days later Lisa calls me. Susan had kept her promise and obtained the phone number of "the best waxer in town." I'm not even sure what that means! Three of us are ready to commit. We call for appointments, but Monica, the lauded waxing expert, is booked weeks in advance. She has one cancellation. We considerately give the opening to Lisa; after all, she has a romantic emergency on her hands. Only two days 'til Vegas. Lisa seems to think we're just a bit *too* happy to hand over the time slot, but desperation drives her, and she takes it.

Aware that we are behaving like teenagers, Susan and I go to the appointment with Lisa. The place looks pretty much like any nail salon from the outside. The gold lettering on the window does mention waxing along with the other services, but unless you were looking for it, you probably wouldn't notice that this place offered mild torture for a price. The receptionist gives us a curious and slightly disapproving look when Susan and I insist we wanted to watch "the procedure."

Once in the room, we stand in the corners to allow enough room for the aesthetician to move around the table, where Lisa, naked from the waist down but for a hankie-sized washcloth placed where Roman and Greek artists used to place the "leaf," lies trying to relax.

"Deep breaths," I say. Lisa and Susan *both* comply.

Soft classical music is playing, no "Girl from Ipanema" for this place. The room smells good, not too sweet, not too musky, a clean scent from candles burning. The gloved technician stirs the wax. Lisa has chosen clear wax. You get to choose the color when you make the appointment. One more customized detail to drive the price up? Monica moves over to the table and leans over Lisa. I'm holding my breath, but not until I hear a slight whimpering from Lisa do I realize I've also closed my eyes. I open one eye and see that Lisa's little triangle of salt-and-pepper hair is now covered in wax. Monica lays strips of paper on top of the wax. "Okay, this will hurt a little." No kidding.

Rip!

"Ow!" That was Susan.

Lisa's lips are clenched shut. Her hands are gripping the sides of the table in a death grip.

Three more rips, and three more flinches from Susan and me, and the deed is done. Lisa no longer has to worry about the color of hair below her waist. Monica is explaining that Lisa will need to repeat the process every twenty to thirty days, depending on her personal growth rate, just like a haircut. Right. Haircuts don't usually make childbirth look relaxing.

By the time we leave the place, Lisa is very happy in that giddy "I survived" sort of way. Susan has made an appointment, and I buy some special touch-up color that I can use to make the hair down there match the hair up here.

Lisa was exuberant at our next Boomer Babes lunch. She said Jeff sent flowers to the wax woman upon returning to Scottsdale. But the other details were too hot to divulge.

"In my sex fantasy, nobody ever loves me for my mind."
—Nora Ephron

Sex and the New Pill: Diane's Story

Viva Viagra!

While most of my stories come directly from personal friends/associates or personal experiences, this particular story comes from a news item. Yes, it made the paper, and not exactly in a good way. But, despite the ending, I still felt it showed a lot of creativity, spunk, and the endless hope of the human heart.

As sunlight filtered through the drawn shades and the air-conditioning whirred on overtime, Diane wished there was more pink in the room. She had read a long time ago that pink made your complexion look younger. However, her visitors were all over fifty, and she could pass for at least ten years younger than that, at least until she went outside into the harsh sunlight and her visitors put their glasses back on.

Diane glanced at the clock on the wall, 10:45 A.M. Her appointment would be showing up soon. Fred was the first client today, as he was every Sunday. He would drop the wife at church, come over, take care of business, and be back to pick up the missus before the church organ sounded its last note.

She flicked on her tranquility fountain. Fred, unlike many of her regulars, didn't have problems with incontinence, so the bubbling water wouldn't bother him. At times she felt more like a caregiver than a sex-for-hire senior.

Back in smoggy L.A., she had made a living as an elementary-school teacher, although even then she occasionally moonlighted as a call girl. Old habits are hard to break. She had put herself through college working as an escort, so the next step came naturally. Heck, she used to sleep around for free, why not get paid for it? She had gotten pregnant at seventeen by some football player, and her mother kicked her out of the house.

In California, most of her johns were executives or CEOs with more money than time. Diane was discreet and very accommodating, no weird request went unfulfilled. But by the time she reached her late forties, most of her clients hit fifty-something and the midlife crisis began. They started to spend long hours in gyms and legit massage parlors; some even went to plastic surgeons. And they unanimously agreed that any woman over thirty was too old for them. Around the same time, two significant things changed in Diane's life: her married daughter got a job and began to drop her five kids off at Diane's place for hours of free babysitting, and real estate prices in Los Angeles hit the ceiling. So Diane, the survivor, quietly arranged for early retirement from her teaching position, put her house on the market and moved to Sun City, Arizona.

She didn't miss the spoiled grandkids and left behind very few friends. She bought a two-bedroom duplex, in a quiet part of town. "Quiet part of town"—heck, this was Sun City. The whole place was as quiet as an empty church, and the streets were always so clean, it reminded her of *The Stepford Wives* (the original with lovely Tina Louise).

No surprise that she quickly became bored. What was surprising is that she decided to take up golf. With her brand-new golf bag and assorted clubs, she joined the flock of women who practiced daily at one of the many local driving ranges. Soon, Diane realized that many of her fellow golfers were widows, and, more important, that there weren't many single men of their age in Sun City. In fact, there weren't many single men of any kind in Sun City. Thus the "casserole brigade."

As soon as a married woman died, word of her demise spread quickly through the community, and dozens of women would show up at the newly widowed man's door bringing trays of lasagna, pans of baked spaghetti, and platters of cold cuts. On the upside, newly widowed men didn't have to worry about cooking for months if they had a big freezer. On the downside, well, Diane wasn't sure there was a downside. She found the whole thing extremely funny, but also fascinating. As *she* wasn't looking for Mr. Right, she could view the whole ritual dispassionately, and she was beginning to suspect the situation represented a business opportunity.

Her suspicions were strengthened by after-golf conversations. The women would linger at the club, for drinks or lunch. Conversation would often work its way around to men. Diane, who had never married, was astonished at how the women would blush when talking about sex or the lack of it. Viagra came up again and again, usually in hushed tones accompanied by soft giggles. It soon became apparent that the blushing and the giggling had to do with their husbands' rediscovered libidos, and not all of them were happy about it. The majority of these retired women preferred the way things were *before* Viagra. The men loved it; the women hated it. Well, not *all* women.

About this same time, Diane stumbled onto another interesting and surprising piece of information. The article was listed under *Odd News* and the headline read, CONDOMS SELL LIKE HOTCAKES IN RETIREMENT COMMUNITIES. Well, *of course* she clicked on it. Turned out the maker of a well-known brand of condoms had held a sales contest. The salesperson with the highest order of condoms for the month would win a cruise to Alaska for two (surely they would also get a supply of free condoms to take along). The kicker? The winning salesperson's territory was none other than Sun City, Arizona. Sun City, where the average age is seventy-five.

Diane mused; most of the men in Sun City are married. Why do they need condoms? Then the epiphany. A clear pattern emerged. Men use Viagra, wives get annoyed and refused sex, men get sex somewhere else, *with protection*. Brilliant. Diane's mind was filled with possibilities.

One day, as much out of sheer boredom and curiosity as a need to make money, she placed an ad under "Personal Ser-vices" in the local newspaper. The ad was cleverly worded; only men over fifty were to call, and the way she touted her magic hands, it was clear that no one should come expecting traditional intercourse, but everyone would leave satisfied.

In no time she had a good little business going. Curious fact: most appointments were on Sundays. These retirees had little in common with her California johns. They had even less personality or maybe it was her, she never was attracted to the men she did business with—though she did remember an unusual size, extremely kinky requests, or particularly exuberant expressions of jubilation at ejaculation. For the most part, they had all been lumped into an odorous haze of Aqua Velva, semen, and pot. In Sun City, the lump smelled of Old Spice, cafeteria food, and Bengay.

A car door slammed and Diane peeked out the window. There was Fred. He had parked his car around back as instructed, good old boy. She didn't want neighbors keeping track of her many regular visitors. By the time she opened the door, everything was ready. The room smelled of vanilla-scented candles, the fountain was making soothing sounds, and the lights were dim. Fred was very matter of fact; he began to undo his belt as he walked toward the den. His cursory manner made Diane imagine how great their sex life must have been for Mrs. Fred. No wonder the Mrs. wasn't happy about Viagra. She probably lit candles of gratitude every day on the altar of his lost sexual performance.

This particular Sunday, Diane had two more Viagra aficionados before five P.M. Then she had Tom. Tom had been a bit of a mystery and a challenge, and he was keeping her interest alive way beyond the business aspect of the situation. The first time he visited her, he only wanted to talk. He paid the full fee. She assumed he couldn't perform and suggested Viagra. He didn't say much, just looked at her with his strange pale blue eyes, so watery she wondered if the man was crying. To her surprise, he came back, and they had sex. Real sex. Tom liked to talk, a lot. She found out his wife of many years was in one of those places for Alzheimer's patients, and his visits to Diane coincided with his visits to his wife. He came to Diane after, as if the sex released his pent-up sorrow, helping him to maintain his sanity. No Viagra needed.

He visited mostly on Sunday nights and Diane got so emotionally dependent on his visits, she encouraged him to stay the night, no extra charge. He never did.

A few months went by, and Tom's wife took a turn for the worse. The call came in on his cell phone while he was with Diane. After he rushed out, Diane had to admit to herself she was enamored with this man and couldn't fathom why. She hated taking money from him. Obviously his wife wasn't going to live much longer, and Diane could be there for him. After a sleepless night, she decided she had to let her johns go and stop doing business so that Tom would understand how special he was to her. Her ad was expiring in a week anyway, and she would not renew it. She had already saved a pretty nice chunk of money for her rainy days, and it never rained in the desert anyway. Yes, it sounded like a wonderful plan. Soon Tom would forget about her little side business, and maybe they could move in together, go golfing, whatever couples did in Sun City. Perhaps she should bake him a chicken enchilada casserole.

Meanwhile, at a desk in the Maricopa County Sheriff's Office, a deputy scratched his head and stared at a puzzling ad in the Sun City newspaper. By its tone, he would have guessed that this was a sex-for-hire ad. But in Sun City? The ad clearly stated that anyone responding must be over fifty. Had to be a prank. Just in case, the deputy mentioned it to his superior, who was nearing retirement age himself. With no hesitation, the sergeant said, "I'd better go out there next Sunday. Check it out." When the deputy looked skeptical, the sergeant chuckled knowingly. "Son," he said, "never underestimate the power of Viagra."

"The most romantic thing any woman ever said to me in bed was 'Are you sure you're not a cop?'"—**Larry Brown**

Body Shop: Julie's Story

Plastic surgery addict tells all.

Here is my version of a story you've possibly already heard as it made the news in a big way. This trailblazer had her own views about love and the pursuit of happiness. Or, as some unknown philosopher once said, "A relationship is what happens between two people who are waiting for something better to come along."

When Jessica's husband #3 filed to end their marriage, under "reasons" he wrote "fraud." In big bold letters. FRAUD. And he didn't file for a divorce like his two predecessors, he asked for an annulment.

"An annulment, can you believe it? Jerk!" Jessica said.

Her friend Julie could believe it; she didn't understand it, but she could believe it. Vance was a great catch; he had looks, money, good manners, and he was a celebrity—a very generous celebrity at that. Julie had been the maid of honor at the wedding, but then she'd been the maid of honor at Jessica's first two ceremonies also. However, this last one was special. Jessica and Vance had been married in Hawaii on the beach at sunset. Vance had hired a private jet to fly the entire wedding party from Los Angeles to Maui, and he also covered everyone's hotel expenses; that was a lot of dough. There they all were, the entire wedding party barefoot on the sandy beach. They had leis around their necks, flowers in their hair. And some observant guest spotted the "green flash" in the sky. That splash of intense emerald light appearing on the horizon just as the sun sets into the ocean is supposed to bring good fortune to the happy couple.

"Julie, are you listening?" Jessica's impatient voice brought Julie back to the present, the two of them having lunch at the posh country club, Vance's posh country club. A silver-haired gentleman walked by their table and nodded at Jessica; her whole face lit up as she said hello in her throaty, sexy voice. *Uh, oh, Jessica is on the prowl again.* She was a resilient one all right.

"Notice the man who just went by?" Jessica smiled, showing her perfect white veneers. "He's filthy rich. I think he really likes me. And I don't mean as a friend . . ." She finished with a suggestive laugh. Julie started to ask if he was single but remembered that was irrelevant with Jessica.

"Jessie, what happened with Vance? I thought you two, were, you know, a perfect match. And the fraud thing, what is it that he thinks you defrauded him of?"

Jessica shrugged, sipped her mimosa. "It's not that kind of fraud." She seemed reluctant to go on, but tried to explain.

"He wants an annulment on the grounds that I, uh, *misrepresented* myself to him."

Julie gasped, the truth dawning on her. "You mean . . ."

Jessica nodded and tried to look bored. "He is saying that I am the product of 'artificial enhancement' and since I'm not the real thing, and because of my 'failure to disclose' our marriage contract is null."

"Real thing? He didn't know about your implants?" Julie had lowered her voice for the last part of that sentence. She couldn't believe she had actually said that. Besides, how was that possible? They hadn't exactly had a chaste courting relationship.

"Oh, honestly Julie, we're talking nips and tucks, little things everybody does to look their best." With her long red acrylic nails she pushed back a lock of frosted hair extension—hair extensions that cost more than one month's mortgage on Julie's condo.

Julie and Jessica had met in high school, both average students with average looks. Julie went on to college and studied to become a teacher. Jessica decided she would become famous, and once Jessica decided something there was no stopping her.

She signed up for modeling classes, and worked nights at a strip joint to pay tuition. After graduating from the modeling school, she went to lots of job interviews but never got the job. Her last modeling interview was for a swimsuit catalog. They told her her breasts were too small. Jessica started to moonlight at a new strip joint and soon she had saved enough money for breast augmentation, as the plastic surgeons like to call it. And a very impressive augmentation it was, because the cost was the same regardless of size. Might as well go really big and get her full money's worth, she thought. She was still popping painkillers when she went back to see the catalog people. Ironically, they told her that now her breasts were too *big* for the swimsuit catalog. However, this crushing news was cushioned (if you'll forgive the pun) by the fact that her new bosom wasn't too big for the catalog publisher. He hired her on the spot as his personal secretary. Jessica couldn't type, file or take dictation, but she had other skills. A few months later when she got pregnant, the catalog publisher became husband #1.

Julie clearly remembered the miserable months of Jessica's pregnancy and the marital fights she had witnessed. Jessica and #1 argued about everything. If one wanted the TV on, the other wanted to read. If he was in the mood for a steak dinner out, she wanted to cook homemade soy stew (her cooking was another sore point, but we'll leave that at that). If #1 wanted desert landscaping, she wanted a lawn. It was the last straw when he hired a new secretary with larger breast implants and real typing skills. Jessica left him *and* the baby two months after giving birth. Cleaned out his bank account and got a nose job.

Jessica always scheduled her surgical procedures in the summer when Julie was off work and could drop Jessica off, pick her up, and wait on her hand and foot for a couple of days. Since Jessica usually chose exotic locales for her fix-ups and footed all the travel expenses, Julie began to look forward to free summer vacations. The summer after Jessica had her nose made more *aristocratic*, she had gotten cheek implants, trying to achieve the cool look of Audrey Hepburn in *Breakfast at Tiffany's*. Then, she'd had her ears pulled closer to her head. Then liposuction on her tush, thighs and ankles. Next, a mini face-lift (she was only twenty-nine!). And there were many more. Julie's favorite was the summer Jessica had a full-face chemical peel. That was pretty: a week of oozing, red skin, followed by a week of crusty peeling, and then several weeks of heavy makeup to cover the damage. For months, every time Jessica went from a cool temperature to a warm one, her face would turn beet red. One evening they were having a glass of wine at an outdoor café in Vancouver, B.C. It was the end of the summer, and there was a soft ocean breeze. Jessica stepped inside to pay the bill, and her face flushed so badly that the M.D. who was behind her in line thought she was terribly ill. He came to the rescue and she wooed him. He became husband #2.

"How are you doing financially?" Julie asked.

"Not well. The Mrs. Lady America lawsuit left me pretty broke. This is not one of my best years," Jessica said, very matter-of-factly, no tears, no choking up.

Driving home, Julie's mind was on Jessica. The two of them had started out as equals, but then Jessica began her trip to fame and fortune. Last year she'd been crowned Mrs. Lady America and met Vance. It seemed she had it made. Well, here they were now: Jessica had lost her crown and was soon to lose Vance. Julie's life didn't seem so inferior anymore. In a few years she would retire with a decent pension plan, a mortgage-free cottage in Sedona, Arizona, and a grown son she could visit in Alaska during the summer (since she suspected the visits to plastic surgeons were about to stop). She thought back on the summers: chin implant, breast redo, tummy tuck, endoscopic brow lift, lower eyelids, full face-lift, lower body lift. Yes, Jessica had reinvented herself to the great beauty that conquered the crown and men's hearts.

Unfortunately, Jessica's divorce was final before the Mrs. Lady America competition was over, and therefore she wasn't techni-cally a "Mrs." Perhaps no one would have noticed except that her divorce from Vance, three months after winning the crown, made national news. Ouch. With big names like the *Star* and the *Enquirer* chasing her, other lies surfaced, like her age, her professional background, and the university degree she had purchased on the Internet.

After lunch, Julie went home, changed into comfortable clothes, and made herself some tea. The early news was on the local channel, and there was Vance—in his three-piece suit, starched shirt, and imported silk tie—pretending to try to avoid the media. He thrived on exposure. They were asking questions about the impending divorce battle. Wait. These people were from Fox, CNN . . . Whoa, he was making the national news again, and dragging Jessica with him.

"When your own child doesn't recognize you . . ." What was Vance saying? Oh, dear God, he was talking about Jessica's daughter. Jessica and the kid had been estranged for years; of course she wouldn't recognize her.

He opened a folder, pointing to something inside. "I've got photos, plastic surgeons' testimony . . ." She had heard enough. She turned off the TV.

Julie was tempted to call Jessie, but what would she say? The phone rang; she recognized Jessie's private line on the caller ID.

"Julie, are you watching channel five?"

"Um, yeah. Well, I was."

"Do you see what he is doing?"

"Divorcing you because of your plastic surgery?"

"Annulment, Julie, annulment, like the marriage never existed so I won't get a penny."

"I'm so sorry, Jessie. What about what's inside you? That's the real thing. Doesn't that count?"

"Forget it. I'm signing with a literary agent and writing a book. *Yesterday's Duckling, Today's Swan*. It will give new hope to every American woman in need of a new look, and I can get product-placement fees from every plastic surgeon who ever worked on me. By the way, I heard there's a new procedure that restores your skin to the elasticity of a twenty-year-old. The surgeon who discovered it is in Monte Carlo. What are you doing in July?"

"July? Well, gosh, I'll be going to Monte Carlo, of course."

"Life is so constructed that the event does not, cannot, will not match the expectation."—**Charlotte Brontë**

The Big O! Pam's Story

How many kinds of big O do you think women talk about?

Pam was my neighbor when my kids were growing up. Because she was a nurse, she was always the first person I called if I had a medical question. Like many women, Pam always put everyone else's needs before her own. Until she finally decided it was time to take some TLC for herself.

By the time their last kid left home for college, Pam had accepted that her husband of twenty-five years was fooling around. For years she had made excuses for the little clues she found: the long, dark hairs on her husband's sport coat must have been from someone in the crowded elevator at his downtown high-rise; the perfume on his shirt was from being accidentally sprayed while walking through a cosmetics department at Nordstrom's. By the time lipstick showed up on his tighty whities, her trained brain told her it must be red ink from a broken pen.

Pam worked at the local hospital as a part-time nurse. Her job eased the pain of empty-nest syndrome and still gave her time to enjoy the kids and grandkids when they came to visit. One Friday morning, as she was walking into the hospital for the start of her shift, her husband called and suggested they meet after work for dinner. He would call her with the name of the restaurant after he made the reservation. Pam suddenly felt very pleased with herself: patience was paying off, and obviously her husband had come to his senses.

His office closed at six. By seven he still had not called about dinner. At nine she drove home, never having heard from her husband and no longer hungry due to the building anxiety. Had he been in a car accident? Where could he be? She waited up, or tried to, and fell asleep watching the *Late Show*. She found his letter on her pillow a few hours later when she dragged herself into the bedroom. In the letter, her husband said he needed solitude in order to "find himself." He said she shouldn't worry about him; he would be in touch as soon as he found inner peace.

Apparently, it didn't take him long and the solitude part was optional. About a week later Pam discovered that their joint savings account had been cleaned out, and a young secretary had gone searching for herself along with Pam's missing husband.

Now the house was emptier than ever, and Pam felt self-conscious at work where everybody kept telling her "how sorry" they were about her situation. She decided to take her talents somewhere else. Soon she landed a job in a plastic surgeon's private practice. How different from her work at the hospital! Here, patients had "elective surgery," and they waited in a reception room filled with flowers, soft music, and signature furniture. No insurance cards were ever pulled from any purses, and all the payment checks had lots of zeros. Pam never took anyone's temperature, didn't check pulses, and never cleaned up body fluids. This was heaven on earth as far as jobs went. The pay was excellent and the hours short, and, most important, all her nights and weekends were free.

The receptionist was a young lady with a foreign accent and large green eyes and a tiny doll face. It turned out the accent was Australian and her green irises were the disposable kind, but Annika's face was indeed as beautiful as a china doll.

When Annika needed a place to live, Pam offered to share her house, and so they became roommates. Annika was much younger than Pam and much more street wise. She was a pleasant and considerate roommate. They carpooled together and did most of their shopping together. It turned out that Annika was older than Pam had assumed, and she had a penchant for men—actually, it was more like a penchant for impulse sex with various men. One at a time, thank goodness.

Annika would bring her date home—usually late at night on a Saturday—and Pam would hear them laughing and whispering, as well as a few gasps and sighs before Annika's bedroom door closed behind them. Fortunately for Pam, the men left early, so she didn't have to bump into strangers while picking up her morning paper. Pam couldn't help noticing that for all of the media hoopla about the shortage of single men over forty, Annika seemed to have a never-ending supply of what she affectionately referred to as her "weekend warriors."

Despite Annika's efforts to be considerate, there were occasions when Pam's sleep was interrupted by loud noises. Noises coming from Annika's bedroom. The first time it happened, it sounded to Pam like the crying of a kitten. Maybe a neighborhood cat was locked out? Just as she was about to put on her robe and go check, the meowing stopped. When she asked Annika about it, Annika wanted to know what it sounded like. Pam tried her best imitation, making her friend laugh very hard. Annika said: "Yes, yes, that's right, that's precisely the way I sound when I orgasm."

Orgasm, the big O word. You've heard about it, you've read about it. Some women have experienced it, and some haven't. Pam was one of those who hadn't. Ever. In a moment of weakness, intrigued by those crying kitten noises in the night again, she confessed to Annika that she had never had cause to mew like a lost cat. It became Annika's life's purpose to get Pam to experience an orgasm. At first, she offered some of her own lovers—only the best, of course. The look of sheer horror in Pam's eyes gave her the answer. Okay, Pam would have to meet her own orgasm-inducing lover.

After much insistence, Annika convinced her to go to a club on a Saturday night. It was then and there that Pam discovered another cruel side of life. She was invisible, and not because of her age, but because everything about her, from her no-style mousy hairdo to her comfortable shoes and khaki pants, screamed dowdy.

Instead of running home to hide, it was a sign of her growing confidence and desire for adventure that Pam not only stayed, but paid close attention to the details setting her apart. There were women there older looking than she who were receiving a healthy dose of flirting and attention. The hausfrau way she dressed was obviously a factor, one easy to fix. But mostly, she decided, it was about attitude.

A little later, Annika let her know she didn't need a ride home. Driving back alone, Pam decided to change her appearance and her attitude. First, she traded her glasses for contact lenses. That was easy and painless. For the first time in her life, people noticed her lovely hazel eyes, and, more important, they complimented her on them—*men* complimented her on them. Next came her hair. She went to Annika's stylist. *That* change wasn't as subtle as the contact lenses. Not only did her hair go from straight, no maintenance, generic shoulder-length blah to a short, pixie cut with flattering fringe around her face, but she let the hairstylist put highlights in it. She walked out of the salon feeling fresh, hip, and ten years younger. At that point, a wardrobe change was a given. It had been a while since Pam had tried on anything with actual sizes. For the last ten years or so, she had bought size medium clothes at inexpensive superstores. Most of her pants had elasticized waistbands, and it was with a sense of shock that she realized she didn't *have* a waist anymore. The old Pam would have said with a sigh, "No wonder my husband ran off with the secretary, I look like a cow."

The new Pam decided to join a gym. But Annika wasn't the patient type, and she was a woman with a mission. She reminded Pam that they worked for a plastic surgeon and a good one, too. To the look of puzzlement on Pam's face, Annika mouthed one word: "Liposuction."

For every one of Pam's objections Annika had an answer. The cost? You work there, you'll get a discount. The money? They take installments, right out of your paycheck. Once she got Pam to agree, Annika decided it was time to celebrate, but she didn't open a bottle of bubbly like most people would. No, Annika ran out and purchased the size-8 dress Pam had tried on but couldn't fit into. The zipper had gone about halfway up and refused to budge. They hung the dress in the entryway where Pam would see it every time she came home or went out.

Pam made arrangements for the lipo. This wasn't as painless as her contacts, and it was certainly more expensive than the new hairstyle, but the results were worth it. She wore the dress for the first time to her thirty-year high school reunion, and for the first time in her adult life she was the life of the party and far from invisible. Good old Chuck, a crush from her sophomore year and newly divorced, asked for her phone number. Pam gave it to him, but on her way home she decided she wasn't going to get involved with someone while she was still on the rebound. The old Pam would have been grateful someone asked her out. The new Pam resolved to take care of herself and wait for the right time.

One day at the office, Pam recognized a patient waiting in the VIP room. A local newscaster. According to Annika, this woman, a TV personality, came every five to six weeks for various types of services. There was Botox for the crow's feet and the frown lines, fat transfer for the smile lines, and collagen for her lips. Pam was astonished. She had watched this woman on the ten o'clock news for about ten years, and she never suspected a thing. "See," said Annika, "I told you we were employed by the best plastic surgeon in town. You can do it, too." In fact, that was exactly what Pam was thinking. She had been going out almost every Saturday night, and although she met nice men and had gone out on dates from time to time, she had yet to meet someone special. She decided to have fun while keeping her eye out for a dreamboat.

The call about her husband came on the day Pam received her first Botox treatment. It was from a police detective. He wanted to ask her some questions regarding her husband. What a shock. It had been over a year since he left her, and she had been so busy and having so much fun that she never bothered to file for divorce. What had he gotten her into now? The detective reassured her that her husband was alive and well, and said he would prefer not to discuss the issue over the phone.

She agreed to stop by his office after work.

Detective Brown didn't look at all the way Pam expected; then again, her knowledge of detectives was limited to reruns of *Colombo*. No trench coat or fedora here, this detective wore a well-tailored sport coat and neatly pressed trousers. He appeared to be in his forties, and Pam got a whiff of aftershave when he closed the door after she entered. She liked this detective a lot better than the TV stereotypes.

Detective Brown seemed genuinely surprised that she had not filed for divorce, and commented, "That probably kept some honest men from asking you out." She smiled lightly and felt a slight blush around her hairline. Brown showed her some photos. She barely recognized her husband: he had gained a lot of weight and had lost a lot of hair—not a good trade-off. Some of the photos showed him with a woman Pam didn't know, but she assumed this was the missing secretary.

Detective Brown told her that the husband, the secretary, and the latter's three-year-old daughter had been living together in a rented house outside of Chicago. Without a job and in need of cash, the couple started making porn and selling it on the Internet. Pam glanced at the photos of the fat and bald man and grimaced slightly.

Detective Brown must have read her mind. "They called themselves Bunny and Claus. He wears a fake white beard. It was live cam, from their own bedroom. People paid a fee to watch. I guess there's no accounting for taste, and none of this is illegal. However, one day while they were doing their 'show,' the little girl woke up from her nap and walked into their room wearing nothing but her birthday suit. They didn't notice her right away. Their camera was still rolling, and suddenly here is a three-year-old girl in the same room where two naked adults are performing sexual acts. We now have child pornography. Someone taped the incident and reported them to the authorities.

I'm not working the case—it's out of state—but we were asked to make sure that there is no past history of child molestation or child abuse."

After she assured Detective Brown that her husband was a loser and a cheat but not a child molester, she added, "What's going to happen to him, to them?"

"I'm not sure. Again, it's not our case. I'll be happy to keep you posted, though. In the meantime, I suggest you get a fast divorce. It's bound to hit the news. With such a quirky twist, the child and the cheaters, the media will have a grand time."

Pam went straight to a friend's house, a friend who happened to be a divorce attorney. By the time Detective Brown called her with an update, she was riding the fast lane to singlehood. He told her that her husband and his mistress were getting off with probation and community service. "It was pretty apparent from the tape that they hadn't meant to involve the little girl in their sleazy business."

Pam was surprised to find that she was relieved. Her ex was a jerk, but he wasn't a sicko. And he was still the father of her children. "Well, thanks. I appreciate your letting me know," she said.

The detective didn't seem eager to hang up. He hemmed and hawed a little bit, and then said, "I was wondering if you'd meet me for drinks after work. Talk about the case, or, ah, you know, just talk."

Pam gladly agreed to meet him.

On their two-week anniversary, Detective Brown, whom she now called John, showed up for their Saturday night date with roses, champagne, a box of chocolate-covered strawberries, and a copy of the *Kama Sutra*. Pam flushed from the top of her head to the tips of her toes, pulled him inside, and kissed him deeply. She just knew that the tingling she felt between her thighs was only the beginning of what was going to be a wonderful, memorable, *historic* night of her life.

What's New Pussycat? Lynn and Tom Jones, That Is.

An unusual Internet meeting; no cats were hurt in the forging of this romance.

Lynn's friend Joyce told me this story. It is the type of story that makes you want to go out and buy a computer to surf the Internet. Some of us possibly already order gifts and prescriptions online. Why shouldn't love be next?

Lynn was skeptical about the computer her son had given her, but in time she came to appreciate some of the things she could do with it, especially e-mail. Now she could get photos of her grandson daily and watch him grow via the Internet. When she heard about the money she could save by ordering prescriptions online she was thrilled. Her friend Joyce taught her how to order online and how to google for information. Lynn's arthritis medications had to be filled every three months. She picked a Canadian online pharmacy. The first time she ordered, she had to fax the actual prescriptions and fill out a questionnaire, but after that, reordering was a breeze. She even had her own personal customer service representative in case she had questions.

According to his e-mail introducing himself, her customer rep's name was Tom, Tom Jones.

The name brought up old memories for her, happy memories of a young, hip singer, loaded with sex appeal. Without pausing to think, she clicked on Reply, typed in "What's new Pussycat?" and watched in horror as her index finger hit Send.

Oh, my gosh . . . here she was, a middle-aged woman, acting

like a silly teenager. What was the poor man going to think? He probably received dozens of silly notes like that from nostalgic romantics every day. The first twenty-four hours following her impulsive gesture she was utterly miserable and felt stupid about the whole thing, but by the next day she had other things on her mind and soon she forgot about it.

Three months later, she renewed her prescription online, carefully avoiding clicking too close to anything with Tom Jones's name on it. Heck, he probably never got the message, she told herself. The firm's spam filter would have taken care of that—even if she had no idea how a spam filter worked.

Not long after sending in her refill, Lynn's birthday rolled around. It was her first post-computer birthday and someone had sent her a cyber birthday card! How exciting. She bet it was from her son. She followed the instructions and retrieved the card.

A cartoon group of cats danced in a circle and sang "Happy Birthday" punctuated by loud "Meow, meow, meows!" The personal greeting read: "What's new pussycat?" It was signed, Tom Jones.

Tom Jones? How did he know it was her birthday? Of course! He would have access to the questionnaire she had filled out for the online service. Lynn hated to admit it, even to herself, but she loved the card. She hadn't felt so excited in years. What now? Should she answer? Darn, she would have to consult Joyce about cyber etiquette.

Joyce became so animated over the phone that she gave Lynn a headache. She ended by saying she'd come right over. Joyce admired the card and the man's pluck. If it *was* a man . . . after all, it could just be a cyber name. There might not even *be* a *real* Tom Jones. Or maybe this was simply a casual greeting he sent to all his customers on their birthdays. And even if he really were flirting just a bit, he might be married, or too young, or too old. They decided to sleep on it.

After tossing and turning for a couple of hours, Lynn got up in the middle of the night, turned on her computer, and sent a thank-you note. And so it began. They exchanged sweet, innocent, chatty e-mails back and forth. His name really was Tom Jones, he was a grandfather, retired, and enjoyed doing this "cyber-concierge" work from the comfort of his own home. And by the way, no, not many people sent him Tom Jones jokes, and he was delighted that Lynn had.

At some point they exchanged phone numbers and moved their relationship into the real world. It was always proper, innocent, and extremely romantic, at least from Lynn's point of view. He had a certain way of pronouncing "Hello" that made her giggle softly, like a silly teenager. The months went by, and their conversation moved to more personal and intimate discussions, but to Lynn's surprise, Tom never asked for her photo, so she never asked for his. They had described themselves for each other: eyes, hair, and such, and she felt like they had known each other forever. She told him about her son, raising him alone. Tom was a widower, with one married daughter and two lovely grandchildren.

That winter her son called and said he had met a charming young lady and sent Lynn a ticket to Chicago so she could meet his fiancée.

"You'll be so close," Tom said.

"I guess I will," she answered, waiting. Hoping for an invitation.

The e-mail came a few days later: if she could spare a day, maybe they could meet halfway, say, in Detroit? For a cup of coffee?

Lynn loved the suggestion, and, in spite of the knot in her stomach, the idea of finally meeting him in person. She told him she would discuss it with her son when she got to Chicago, and maybe borrow the car for a day. The details of her trip were discussed both by mail and by phone, but he never mentioned the halfway rendezvous again, and she was too shy to bring it up.

Joyce drove her to the airport and teased her the whole way about not losing this opportunity to meet Tom. Lynn assured her she had his phone number, and she could call him if she wanted to. The discount ticket had her change planes in Norwalk, with a two-hour layover. She didn't mind. This was the first time her son had sent a plane ticket; obviously it meant a lot to him that she meet his fiancée. Besides, she had plenty of reading material. The waiting lounge was empty in the middle of the day, so she bought a cup of coffee and made herself comfortable. Two hours would go by fast.

But she was restless; Norwalk was close to Tom's hometown. What was she thinking? Still, when would she ever get another chance like this? She glanced at her watch. Should she call him? She forced herself to go back to her book.

A few people had begun to wander into the waiting area, and someone sat down next to her. She kept her eyes glued to her book. She didn't want to encourage a conversation, there was too much going on in her head. The coffee gone, she crushed the paper cup and debated getting up and walking around, but she didn't feel like dragging her carry-on. She stared out the large windows, into the gray Eastern skies. The man next to her cleared his throat, but Lynn hardly noticed.

"Hello."

Lynn's head swung around abruptly. That voice! The voice that always made her giggle softly on the phone. She didn't giggle now. When she recovered from her shock, she said: "Tom?"

"Lynn." He nodded, taking hold of her hands. "Just figured I'd keep you company while you wait. Heck, when else are we going to be so close? Geographically, I mean," he added with a twinkle in his blue eyes.

He was everything like she had hoped for, and he felt the same way about her. Now they live happily together in Canada.

"Why not seize the pleasure at once? How often is happiness destroyed by preparation, foolish preparation!"—**Jane Austen**

Welcome to America:
Denise's Story

Deni rescues strays—the two-legged kind.

I met Deni after she retired. I sold her the house where she planned on spending her golden years and where she indulges her compassionate side by taking in stray cats and dogs. Lately, she is also extending her helping hand to young male immigrants, giving new meaning to the old saying, "Welcome to America, land of opportunity."

By forty-three, Deni felt ready to retire. After eighteen years as a lawyer, she received a modest inheritance and decided to store away her briefcase and live modestly. Right off the bat, she resolved to use her time doing as little as possible. She spent days discovering soap operas and the many flavors of potato chips. Deni had been married and divorced once, many years ago, and had worked as an immigration attorney, learning Spanish in the process. She lived in a small home full of charm in an upscale neighborhood and knew very little about gardening, cooking or other stay-at-home delights.

One sunny day, while channel surfing between soaps, she stumbled on a special program about the local animal shelter. A dozen wet tissues later, Deni decided to volunteer there. Because she was such a softy, she ended up taking home many of the unadoptable cats and dogs she cared for. Soon her yard and her home were a wreck, with cats and dogs running amok, jumping fences, and pooping anywhere and everywhere. At night, the slightest noise set off cacophonous barking that kept her and the rest of the neighborhood from getting any sleep. Then one of her rescued Great Danes (yes, there was more than one) managed to get through a locked gate into the neighbor's backyard to rumble with their Saint Bernard—at least that was what she thought at the time.

Many threats of lawsuits, veterinarian fees, and one litter of Great Bernards later, Deni knew that the midnight visit was more amorous than aggressive. But still, something had to give. She had to bring her pet population under control or move. She decided to stay put and managed to find good homes for all of her pets, keeping only one cat, and Houdini, the passionate Great Dane, for herself.

By this time, Houdini was a father, and his offspring were bouncing and running about in the backyard next door. The gate had been fixed to withstand any dog's attempt at escape, but Houdini was not so easily outfoxed, and he simply dug under the gate in order to pay a visit to his brood.

Never one to do things halfway, Houdini dug so deep that part of the fence collapsed. Deni had to keep Houdini inside 24/7 (with brief, supervised potty breaks) until the fence was repaired. Understandably, this gave her great motivation to get it repaired quickly.

Unable to find someone to do the job ASAP, she felt compelled to do what she had vowed never to do; hire an undocumented worker from the street corner. It helped that she spoke the language. Perhaps due to a guilty conscience, she hired the first man to approach the car window. Deni drove Juan to her house. She borrowed tools from everyone on her street, pointed to the pile of wood she had purchased at Home Depot, and asked Juan to fix the fence. Houdini watched it all from the living room window. So did Deni. As he worked, Juan was focused, skillful . . . muscular.

Whoa! Where did that come from? Deni shook off her trance and took Juan a tall pitcher of ice water and a disposable glass. Then she went back into the house to watch her soap operas. But her mind kept going back to the hired help. And her eyes followed her mind. She could see him from her perch on the couch. Juan was in his late twenties or early thirties. He wore clean jeans and a long-sleeved white cotton shirt. A red bandana kept the sweat from his eyes. She couldn't see his face, but she remembered his eyes, dark brown with golden speckles. The shirt was getting damp with sweat and clinging to his body.

"Okay, girl, get a grip. This is getting way too personal." She shifted her position on the couch so she couldn't see him.

In the early afternoon Deni took Juan a ham and cheese sandwich, some chips, and more ice water. He gave her a grateful smile, and she invited him to sit in on the back porch and take a break. Juan told her he would need some fast-setting concrete to reinstall the gate. She said she'd go get it.

Deni sat down and watched him eat his lunch. She had to fight her impulse to ask personal questions; Juan kept the conversation light and neutral. When he went back to work on the fence, Deni left to get the concrete.

Deni spent forty-five minutes looking at a dozen different kinds of concrete. She read each of the packages. She read again. She finally narrowed it down to one of three types and purchased two bags of each type; she'd simply return the wrong ones. With her back bumper nearly grazing the ground under the weight of the concrete in the trunk, she drove home under a dark sky.

Dark skies and rain are as common in Phoenix as Midwestern values in L.A. And most of the time, a dark sky doesn't mean rain; it means dust—as in a dust storm. But this time, the rain began to pour, hard and heavy. All the parched creatures of the desert sent a chorus of thanks toward the sky. Except Deni. She cursed the meteorologist who neglected to forecast the storm. She parked the car in her garage and ran to the backyard. There was Juan, soaking wet, working on the fence, a big grin on his face.

"Dear God, come to the porch," Deni said, as lightning flashed in the sky. "Hurry, you'll get electrocuted." Juan walked over, shaking his hair the way Houdini did after a bath. His shoes made squishy, squashy noises, and around his neck she saw a gold chain with a small cross he wore under his shirt. But Juan was only concerned about not being able to finish the job: you can't pour concrete in the rain.

"You can finish tomorrow," she said. "Come inside and I'll get you a towel." She guided him to the bathroom, gave him a towel and an oversize white terry bathrobe, and ordered him to give her his wet clothes. He hesitated, a look of uneasiness in his golden eyes. Then he obeyed. While the freshly cleaned clothes tumbled in the dryer, she made sandwiches. But instead of ice water she decided the occasion called for a couple of Coronas. *What occasion?* She dismissed her own question. Deni didn't hear Juan walk into the kitchen. He was barefoot, with the robe belted tight around his body, almost as a defense mechanism. He avoided her eyes.

"Juan, are you afraid of me?"

He shook his head in denial. "I'm not afraid. I'm mostly surprised by your kindness." Houdini picked that specific moment to bark at a low-flying bird, and she remembered the lesson of the animal shelter: *Don't get too close, don't get too personal.* They sat on the low couch, ate sandwiches and chips, drank Corona, and talked in Spanish. Memories of the animal shelter and the consequences became less and less vivid in Deni's mind as she listened to Juan's melodious voice and beautiful accent.

It had been a long time since she had spent so much time alone with a man, she thought, and it felt good. She decided she should start going out more, maybe even try Internet dating instead of spending so much time watching soap operas.

Houdini decided he also liked Juan and wanted to play with him. They wrestled like two big teenage boys, Houdini growling and pulling and Juan pretending he couldn't get away from him. Juan was ready to give up and come back to the safety of the couch, but Houdini had other ideas. He clamped his teeth on Juan's robe just as he stood up and the robe came open, and there stood Juan, his exposed manhood inches from Deni's face. She looked up and met Juan's eyes. At first, he looked like a deer caught in the headlights; then his expression changed subtly.

Silence, complete silence. She looked down again and saw

that Juan's eyes weren't the only part of his body that was bigger. *How much more awkward could this get?* she thought, while her hand, as if totally disconnected from the rest of her body, softly explored his growing penis.

The rest happened so quickly that although *safe sex, vaginal cream, and stranger danger* all flashed through her mind, nothing could stop the natural progression.

It took two more days to finish the fence. By daytime Juan was the diligent hired help, but when the sun went down, her bedroom became the set of the best telenovella bodice-ripping scenes one can imagine. When the fence was done, she paid him the established amount for a job well done and drove him back to the same corner where she had picked him up three days earlier. She gave him the address of a construction company that was hiring and legal advice about getting a work visa. He was grateful. So was she. She still couldn't sit comfortably.

Deni went back to her soaps and her chips, and every time she looked at her fence, she thought about Juan and craved sex in the worst way. After a few months, she noticed that her kitchen floor looked dated and dingy. She could sure use some new tile. Yes, new tile sounded more and more like what she needed.

On a sunny early morning she got in her car and drove to the street corner where the undocumented immigrants waited to be hired. She wore lipstick, and this time she looked before hiring.

Years have gone by, and when you visit Deni's home and ask her about the extensive and beautiful remodeling that she's done, she is happy to tell you all about the different projects. There is Pablo's kitchen, Ramon's barbecue (an especially lengthy and involved project), Jesse's gazebo, and, of course, Juan's fence. Every time she mentions a name, Houdini's ears perk up; then he grumbles and goes back to sleep.

Five Celebrity Baby Boomer Trailblazers

Celebrities setting the pace for their less
well-known brethren.
(*Listed by birth date*)

Cher

Birthday: May 20, 1946

Trailblazer Qualities: A more perfect trailblazer would be hard to find; even her ethnic background is unique. She is part Cherokee, part Armenian, and a few more parts from both parents' sides. To date, Cher is the only female singer to have solo top-10 hits in the '60s, '70s, '80s, and '90s. Her song "Believe" was the best-selling single of 1998 and made Cher the oldest woman (fifty-two at the time) to have a #1 hit. And that's only the highlights of her singing career. She also has a long list of achievements as an actress. In 1987 she won an Academy Award for Best Actress in *Moonstruck*. She has also been the recipient of a Grammy, an Emmy, and three Golden Globes.

Trivia: Did you know that Cher made *Guinness World Records* as the top-grossing tour by a female performer for her 2002–2005 concerts? She was also the first female to show her belly button on TV, which in 1975 was a pretty bold move.

Love Life: Even decades after their stormy breakup, Sonny and Cher are still one of the most celebrated musical duos. Cher's devotion to Sonny was obvious, but she never stood in the shadows. If anything she became the more outspoken and outrageous one in their partnership. In 1975, Cher married rock star Gregg Allman, but the two divorced two years later. In the mid-80s, she had a highly publicized romance with Rob Camiletti, who was nearly twenty years her junior. Cher was a "cougar" before the term was even invented.

Ivana Trump

Birthday: February 20, 1949

Trailblazer Qualities: Whoa, where do we begin? Ivana Zelnickova was born in Gottwaldov, Czechoslovakia, now a part of the Czech Republic. She entered the United States through Canada. In 1976 she moved to New York to promote the Montreal Olympics. That same year she met Donald Trump. They married in 1977 and had three children: Donald Jr., Ivanka, and Eric.

Ivana took on major roles in the Trump organization. She became the vice president of Interior Design for the company and was later appointed president of the Taj Mahal Hotel and Casino. Ivana was named Hotelier of the Year in 1990.

When rumors began to circulate that Donald was having an affair with Marla Maples, Ivana confronted Maples on the Aspen ski slopes, which was reported in the *New York Post*. It is rumored that Ivana received $20 million, the $14-million family estate in Connecticut, a $5-million housing allowance, all of her jewelry and partial use of Mar-A-Lago, the family home in Palm Beach, as part of the divorce settlement; a lot more than the prenuptial agreement called for. Not bad for a woman who hardly spoke English when she married "The Donald." But she didn't stop there. She created her own business empire, wrote books, developed lines of clothing, fashion jewelry, and beauty products. Ivana is presently involved in a trademark dispute with

Donald regarding the use of her name associated with real estate services.

Trivia: Ivana Trump became a grandmother when Vanessa Haydon Trump, wife of Donald Jr., gave birth to a girl, Kai Madison Trump, on May 12, 2007.

She has been married four times to Donald's three.

Ivana played a cameo role in the film *The First Wives Club* with the memorable line: "Remember girls, don't get mad, get everything."

Ivana was the host of Oxygen's reality-dating series *Ivana Young Man* in 2006.

Love Life: There is no doubt that Donald Trump, although not her first husband, was Ivana's great love. Since their divorce, instead of feeling sorry for herself, she appears to be competing against him on every playing field: life, business, relationships. They've both remarried multiple times since their divorce. Donald's latest wife is a model from Slovenia, Melania Knauss, twenty-four years his junior. Ivana's new husband is Rossano Rubicondi, a model from Italy, twenty-three years her junior.

Oprah Winfrey

Birthday: January 29, 1954

Trailblazer Qualities: Not only is Oprah the undisputed queen of daytime TV, she changes lives; she brings hope where there is none. She makes things happen. She is the first black female billionaire in world history. *The Oprah Winfrey Show,* which she hosts and produces, has won multiple Emmy Awards. Winfrey also publishes two magazines: *O, The Oprah Magazine* and *O at Home.* She cofounded the women's cable television network Oxygen.

Time named her one of the one hundred people who most influenced the twentieth century. And *Life* listed Winfrey as both the most influential woman and also the most influential black person of her generation. She has invested over $40 million and much of her own time to build and run the Oprah Winfrey Leadership Academy for Girls near Johannesburg, South Africa.

And let's not forget that 49 million U.S. viewers watch her talk show, which airs in 117 countries worldwide. I think we all get the idea.

Trivia: Winfrey was born to unwed teenagers, and Winfrey herself gave birth at the age of fourteen but the baby died shortly afterward.

During a visit at Graceland, Oprah told Lisa Marie Presley that her own grandmother's last name was also Presley.

Winfrey had her DNA tested in 2006, and her genetic makeup was determined to be 89 percent sub-Saharan African. She is also part Native American and East Asian.

Love Life: Winfrey dated movie critic Roger Ebert and reporter Lloyd Kramer. There are other juicy love reports but they are all part of her younger years. For the last twenty years she has been quietly and faithfully sharing her life with Stedman Graham. Not a trailblazer's trait? On the contrary, she could date whomever she wants, but she chooses not to. And she obviously doesn't need a signature on a piece of paper to make their relationship committed.

Ellen DeGeneres

Birthday: January 26, 1958

Trailblazer Qualities: Ellen's entire career has been a series of risks and reinvention. In 1986, DeGeneres was invited to perform on the *Tonight Show* and was the first comedienne ever to be asked over to the couch to visit with Johnny Carson. She made television history again in 1997 on *Ellen*, as the first openly lesbian character on network television.

Known for her wit and fearlessness, soon after 9/11 she quipped: "We're told to go on living our lives as usual, because to do otherwise is to let the terrorists win, and really, what would upset the Taliban more than a gay woman wearing a suit in front of a room full of Jews?"

In September 2003, DeGeneres launched her daytime television talk show. Amid a crop of several new talk shows hosted by celebrities that year, *The Ellen DeGeneres Show* has consistently risen in the Nielsen Ratings and continues to receive widespread critical praise. It's the first talk show in television history to win the Emmy for Outstanding Talk Show for its first three seasons on the air.

Trivia: In May 2006, DeGeneres made a surprise appearance at the Tulane University commencement in New Orleans. Following former U.S presidents George H.W. Bush and Bill Clinton to the podium, she came out in a bathrobe and furry slippers. "They told me everyone would be wearing robes," she said.

DeGeneres is the first openly gay or lesbian person to have hosted the Academy Awards.

Love Life: DeGeneres's relationship with former *Another World* actress Anne Heche turned into material for the tabloid press. The couple broke up and Heche went on to marry male cameraman Coley Laffoon. DeGeneres then had a relationship with actress/director/photographer Alexandra Hedison. They appeared on the cover of the *Advocate* (ironically, after their split-up had already been announced to the press). Since 2004 DeGeneres has been in a relationship with *Arrested Development* and *Ally McBeal* star Portia de Rossi. DeGeneres and de Rossi currently live in Santa Barbara with two dogs and three cats.

Demi Moore

Birthday: November 11, 1962

Trailblazer Qualities: In the 1990s, Moore was the highest-paid actress in Hollywood. She had a string of box-office successes, including *Ghost*, *A Few Good Men*, *Indecent Proposal*, and *The Hunchback of Notre Dame*, for which she was the first actress to reach the $10-million salary mark. In August 1991, Moore, while seven months pregnant, appeared nude on the cover of *Vanity Fair* sparking wide coverage and controversy. Moore shaved off all her long hair on camera, leaving her head totally bald for the movie *G.I. Jane*. She had breast implants done for the movie *Striptease*. Before leaving her self-imposed retirement and returning to the movies, Moore underwent extensive cosmetic surgery including additional breast implants, numerous collagen injections, liposuction, cheek implants, an eyelid life, and a procedure to lift sagging skin around her knees.

Trivia: Demi Moore got her real name, Demetria, from a beauty product her mother saw in a magazine.

In high school, her schoolmates included Red Hot Chili Peppers frontman Anthony Kiedis and actor Timothy Hutton.

She is a passionate raw foodist or live-vegan.

Love Life: Moore married for the first time in 1980, before she was eighteen. She and Freddy Moore divorced in 1985, but she kept his last name. In 1987 she met Bruce Willis and they were married two months later. During their thirteen-year marriage they had three daughters: Rumer, Scout LaRue, and Tallulah Belle. Moore and Willis announced that they were ending their marriage in June 1998. Their divorce was finalized in October

2000. Unlike most Hollywood divorces, theirs was quiet and private.

Moore remarried for the third time in 2005. Her latest husband is actor Ashton Kutcher, seventeen years her junior. They often socialize with Bruce Willis; a big, happy family.

The Lovers

The Lovers

"The Eskimo has fifty-two names for snow because it is important to them; there ought to be as many for love."—**Margaret Atwood**

Tonight is movie night and the Boomer Babes had all agreed to meet at my house. I had imagined a laidback evening—casual chitchat among friends, flowing bubbly, generous portions of cheese and assorted munchies. Tonight we got together earlier than usual to watch *When Harry Met Sally.* Though we've all seen it many times, we have fun watching it as a group.

Kathy and Michelle make a dramatic entrance together. They wear low-cut tops, tight designer jeans, sparkling jewelry, and the mandatory spiky heels, or as Sam calls them: Cinderella slippers for Boomer Babes.

Soon the rest of the group trickles in. Even Lisa joins us since Jeff is away on a business trip. I fill our glasses with sparkling wine and propose a toast to movie love.

"Shouldn't it be love of movies?" Kathy asks.

"No, I mean how movies portray love and lovers. Don't you think that even now, when we're all over forty, we still want the kind of romance we see in the movies?"

By this time, Sam, wearing full NASCAR regalia, strides in and hears my question. She has come directly from the Phoenix International Raceway. After hours of roaring engines hammering her ears, her voice is a bit loud. "Girl," she says, "I love *Days of Thunder,* but you know what I like even more? Paul Newman. I don't care how old he is, he should have been in that movie. He still sizzles!"

I watch Michelle roll her eyes. "Sam," she says, "you like fast cars and fast men. But Paul Newman is a devoted husband, so he hardly qualifies as a fast man." She pauses, then continues, "You're in love with his image."

"So what?" Kathy jumps in. "We all have to start somewhere. Like it or not, we all judge a book by its cover. I bet we pass up a lot of good men because we're not attracted to their looks."

"Whoa, she is so right! I have this thing about facial hair; I would not date a man with facial hair." Susan, the least talkative of the bunch, says, "I connected with this guy on the Internet and we had a real good time chatting back and forth, and seemed very compatible. We exchanged photos, and I was totally bummed when I saw he had a beard. The poor man sent me a new picture of himself without the beard; he shaved it for me. But it was too late; something was gone and couldn't be put back. I know, it makes me a shallow person, but I can't help it—looks do matter."

"We're getting off track here. I'm talking about feelings and emotions. I'm talking the type of love more than the type of lover."

Sam is looking at me in a so-that's-what's-eating-you-up kind of way. "How long since you've gotten laid?" she asks me. I feel my eyes growing bigger and bigger, taking over my whole face. They all start laughing and Lisa throws a pillow at me. Rather than getting into a discussion, I decide it's time to take charge and I click on the remote to start the movie rolling.

"Look at how young Billy Crystal was, and the hair. Do you think it's his hair?" Kathy asks.

"It is if he paid for it." Sam is practical as usual.

We all agree that we love Meg Ryan's flawless face, although we still haven't forgiven her for divorcing Dennis Quaid. We adore Dennis, the quintessential bad boy with a heart of gold. How can we forget him in *The Big Easy*? Michelle is thrilled that his new real-life wife is a real estate person; Michelle claims he shows good taste.

We sigh as we watch the part where the older couples share the secrets of their long unions. Deep down inside, we are all still searching for our soul mate. Michelle's favorite clip is the one with the Asian couple—the man does all the talking while the wife keeps nodding and looking straight ahead. Believe it or not, Michelle gets misty-eyed; tonight a little more than usual.

We all clap and holler at the fake big-O scene—although we each swear *we* never fake it. And every time Carrie Fisher's character says "He'll never leave his wife," we act like a chorus line as we point at poor Susan who gets annoyed but pretends she doesn't.

As the credits roll, Lisa says, "Do you girls ever miss the younger years? You know, when we all thought the world was our oyster?"

"Are you talking about life in general or men in particular?" Susan asks.

"Men, love, sex, relationships. I don't know about you, but I can still remember when I would walk into a room and like the cliché goes, men would undress me with their eyes."

"Yeah, now I could be naked and I doubt they'd notice me at all," says Kathy, who is a striking beauty who could pass for a model.

"I don't think it has to do with our looks; it's that the whole social scene has changed. When I was in my twenties, I wouldn't have dreamed of asking a man out," Michelle says.

"You ask men out now? Good girl."

"No, I don't ask men out, I meant that today's twenty-something girls don't hesitate to ask a man out."

"Hey," Sam speaks with an attitude, "screw the twenty-somethings! Anything they can do, we can do better." We laugh and clink our glasses.

"Actually, she has a point," says Kathy, "there is a lot to be said for experience."

"If you had a magic wand and you could create the perfect lover, what would he be like?" I ask.

"Good in bed." That's Sam, of course.

"Single, without facial hair," says Susan, winking at us.

"Caring." This is from Michelle, spoken almost in a whisper.

"I am lucky to already have my dream lover," Lisa says.

"Dependable, honest, with a sense of humor, in good shape—"

"Stop, stop," Sam says to Kathy, "your lover sounds—perfectly boring. What would you want?" she asks me.

"All of the above," I say. "But really, it's hard to describe a perfect lover, he must have that little extra, that little *je ne sais quoi* that makes your heart race, makes you want to grab on and never let him go."

"You are sooo romantic."

"By the way," Sam says, "did anyone notice what no one listed?"

"What?"

"Money. None of us mentioned that as part of the list. Hmmm." For a minute we all are silent. "I know," says Lisa. "We all want our own money. I don't care how wealthy my man is, I feel a lot more comfortable knowing I have my own money. Don't you?" For once we all agree.

"So," I ask, "if you had to sum up your sex life in one word, I mean your whole sexual history, in one word, what would it be? Anyone?"

"Fear." Sam says the word without hesitation, and we are all stunned. Fear coming from Sam is a pretty big word. "Here's the way I look at it. When I first had sex, I was so young, and all I could think about was how I was afraid of getting pregnant. Then comes the pill and the sexual revolution. Guess what? I was afraid of getting AIDS. Don't look away, you know I'm right, we've all been there. And now? Now I'm afraid of not getting any." She pauses. We are silent for a minute, then roar about "not getting any."

"I can't believe this conversation. We start out talking about which type of lovers we like and now we're talking about fear."

We all munch pensively on our cheese and crackers.

"I don't know about you," Lisa says, glancing sideways at her Blackberry. We all know she and Jeff are text messaging like high schoolers but pretend not to notice. "I've been in love, and out of love, and now I'm in love with Jeff. Sure a great love is wonderful, but even lousy love beats no love. I'm sold on love, I'll take it any way I can."

"I second the motion," says Sam.

They drift out after the news, and I sit alone on the couch staring at the TV. Jay Leno walks out on stage to greet his audience. He is a successful boomer and has been happily married to Mavis for many years. I wonder if they've found the secret of perfect love. Perfect love sounds like an oxymoron, but in reality, is it not everyone's ultimate quest?

If someone asked me to draw a picture of how I see a typical lover, I would draw a horse with blinders on. Why? Because it appears that what these lovers are after is a specific passion—sometimes romantic, sometimes parental, sometimes humanitarian—only focused straight ahead, oblivious to what surrounds them, unable to notice or acknowledge anything but that passion.

So, while we are all lovers to some degree, we often mess up our good intentions because we are chasing illogical results. But when everything works out perfectly, well, we forget all the bad and tell ourselves it was well worth the risk.

Love Me Tender—Love Me True

A Quiz

1. What's your definition of love?

   a. A warm and fuzzy feeling.

   b. A cosmic experience.

   c. A relationship with someone.

   d. Can't imagine what love is like at this point in my life.

2. If asked to describe the different aspects of love you would:

   a. Run out of fingers to count them.

   b. List emotional first, physical next, and everything in between in order of importance.

   c. Say it's hard to pinpoint; somehow, one's capacity for love greatly expands with age.

   d. There is more than two types of love? Like what? Your love interest and your family?

3. Since you've been living alone, your most important emotional investment has been in:

   a. Your grandchildren, followed by their parents.

   b. Your best friend and your absentee grown children, not necessarily in that order.

   c. Your pet, your family, and your friends.

   d. Your housekeeper and your bank account.

4. If asked to name the woman who represents the ultimate lover, your choice would be:

  a. This is hard. So many women are wonderful human beings, always ready to give, I can't pick just one.

  b. Mother Teresa of Calcutta.

  c. Samantha from *Sex and the City*.

  d. Yourself. You've loved your kids, your three former spouses, your job, and now you love doing nothing with great passion.

5. Have you ever experienced true love outside of a romantic relationship?

  a. Of course.

  b. Maybe, I'm not sure.

  c. I've experienced true love, but only in a romantic relationship.

  d. What's true love?

6. If asked to pick between a steamy, intoxicating brief affair and a long comfortable relationship, which would you pick?

  a. In your experience, all relationships start out as steamy and intoxicating.

  b. You'd probably go for the brief, steamy one. Live for today!

  c. What's wrong with having both?

  d. Neither, it takes too much energy and time to be in a relationship. How about a one-night stand? That way, no one is disappointed.

7. If your grown child told you that he or she is more interested in the pursuit of success than that of a lover, you would say:

a. "Pursuing success is good practice; it is foreplay for bigger passions."

b. "Success is as much of an aphrodisiac as sex."

c. "They can't fool me, success is just the road less traveled."

d. "Good, that way I won't need to help change diapers for my grandkids."

8. It is said that we are all born lovers. If that's the case, why do you think so many people are unhappy about their love situation?

a. Perhaps they are not very realistic and see love as a cure-all.

b. Love is such a romanticized subject, but often doesn't live up to our expectations.

c. We are always chasing what we don't have and we fail to appreciate what we do have.

d. That's only true of young, foolish people, not us boomers—we know better.

9. How would you describe most of your friends?

a. Dependable, easygoing, quite enjoyable.

b. Fascinating, entertaining, super people.

c. Not boring, often fun to be with.

d. Who needs friends? I'm surrounded by total losers.

Your Score

Each A answer is worth 6 points. Each B answer is worth 4 points, every C answer is worth 2 points, and D answers are worth no points.

If your score is 48 or over, you are well adjusted in the love department—and not just physical love. You appear to be a very caring, very loving person, always ready to help and to put yourself out there. I bet you find yourself always surrounded by people as nice as you are.

Score between 40 and 48? Whoa! You do take life in by big gulps! You are full of goodwill and enthusiasm. Perhaps too much enthusiasm! Love is good, love is grand, just be careful: you don't want to get burned because of your good intentions.

If you scored less than 40, perhaps you have issues with people or situations surrounding you. It could be that you grew tired of giving and decided to step back. That's all right, sometimes we need a break from things, even from love. Hope you find the path back very soon.

If you had more than five D responses, you are either self-centered or you got burned so badly that you stopped believing. Don't give up, you never know when lightning will strike; the road to newfound happiness may be just around the corner, so keep searching.

As you reflect on the type of lover you are, consider these two quotes from Robert Anthony:

"If you force someone to change, they will lie to you."

"Really loving someone is making it okay for them to be who they are."

Everlasting Love

No batteries required.

There are many kinds of love; we've established that. Now we're going to talk about the kind we all dream of: love that transcends time, physical attraction, and even death. I hope this story will give you a glimpse into such a powerful love. Here is Michelle's story.

Lisa is getting married. It wasn't a big surprise to any of us; I mean, we coached her through her romance's shaky beginnings. Some of us even made the extreme sacrifice of giving up some of our hair—down there—for moral support. Still, here we are over at Michelle's place, eyes misty, reminiscing about . . . everything.

The wedding is months away, but we, her Boomer Babe buddies, want to do something special for this occasion. She's the first one of us to get legally hitched, or rehitched, and believe it or not, we feel traumatized by it.

Michelle, who is a Realtor, offered her newly acquired digs for the first get-together of the wedding planning committee.

Her place is a large two-bedroom condo on the seventh floor of a new downtown high-rise. It was billed as having a water view, but this being the desert and the center of the city, our fantasy architects are still working on that little detail. Regardless, the place is beautiful and the walls of glass offer a fabulous evening view. The star-filled sky mingles with the lights of planes landing and taking off, and the whole scene looks like a well-choreographed ballet of lights.

"Holy shit." That's Sam, of course. Her voice is coming from inside the pantry. We all turn to see what got her attention. "You must be a Virgo," she says to Michelle. Now we're all really curious about what's hiding in that pantry.

Sam is motioning us to come over and take a peek. Crowding the tall, narrow, glass door to the pantry, our gaze follows Sam's accusing finger. There, on a shelf in plain view, is a row of soup cans. We still don't understand Sam's outrage. She taps her finger on the label of the first can: "Alphabet Soup." So? Now her finger travels to the next ones, "Beef and Barley," then "Clam Chowder." Holy shit is right! Michelle's cans are lined up in alphabetical order! Can't wait to see her wine collection.

We are all looking at poor Michelle, our mouths open but silent having finally confronted something unusual enough to stop our blabbering.

"What? I like to be organized. It makes life easier." Michelle sounds defensive. "And yes, I happen to be a Virgo. So what?" Sam walks over and gives Michelle a quick hug; we all relax and head into the living room. I don't think I've ever seen Sam so touchy-feely. What's going on here?

"Sam, please tell, are you into astrology?" Susan asks.

"Sort of. I don't mean astrology for the masses like your daily horoscope; I do my own horoscope on my computer. In fact I was thinking about doing a sign compatibility chart for the happy couple. What do you think?"

"Could be tricky," I say. "What if the odds are against them?"

"Well, I could rig the results," she gives a quick glance at the kitchen area where Michelle is applying her culinary skills to a large salad, "but I wouldn't. Maybe I'll sneak a preview before I share any results with them. Virgos are known to be perfectionists you know," she says half smiling and looking at Michelle. We agree with that and move on to the next subject.

The whole kitchen-living-dining-great room in Michelle's place is filled with the wonderful aroma of her cheese casserole, warm, crusty bread already cooling on the counter, and, although she hardly drinks, a nice array of wines. Her home is decorated in a semi-contemporary flair, with a few unique, antique pieces thrown in. Very cosmopolitan. She owns some interesting artwork. One very large portrait of a man stands out among the paintings. It is done in shades of gray, darker on the top so that you imagine more than you can actually see of the silver hair and pleasant, older face.

"Is it a relative?" I ask between bites of sourdough bread.

"My husband," Michelle says.

"You keep that fancy portrait of your ex in your living room?"

"He died." Though this is said in a whisper, you can feel the pain in those two words.

"I'm so sorry, Michelle, I had no idea." She waves her hand as if to say, *It's okay.* But her whole expression says the opposite. Whatever happened, it definitely wasn't okay. The rest of the group catches the mood and suddenly we begin to talk about a husband who was instead of a husband to be.

"We were together twelve years," Michelle says. "Twelve marvelous years." She utters the sentence with extreme tenderness. "I miss him so much."

The oven's buzzer goes off, and Michelle strolls to the kitchen, puts on big oven mittens, and leans down to check the casserole. We sit there quietly sipping our wine, not sure if she wants to talk about the dearly departed or if she'd rather drop the subject. She brings in a melted, bubbly cheese casserole that is wonderful. We dip, munch, and fight over who gets the larger morsels. We all want the recipe.

"It was John's recipe," Michelle says. Ouch, we did it again. It's a mystery how we went so long without ever hearing about this guy and now he pops up every other sentence! We may as well bring it out in the open and be done with it.

"Michelle, is he Preston's dad?" I ask.

"No. I was married before, when I was very young, to my high school teacher."

"What?" We sound like a chorus, and we are all in a state of shock. "Your high school teacher?"

Michelle shrugs; she's heard these questions before, obviously. "I was eighteen and no, he didn't take advantage of me. My mother was a raging alcoholic, and I don't remember my dad at all. Phillip was our music teacher, always sweet and gentle. I had a terrible crush on him. On prom night, I told him I needed a ride home, and when we got there, before he had time to react, I kissed him—a real open-mouth kiss. I had been practicing on the back on my hand." She smiles to herself, then laughs and says, "It's a long story, you're sure you want to hear this?"

Do we want to hear this? We assure her she won't get us out of her place until she tells us the whole story. We open a new bottle of wine, knock off our shoes, and sit back to listen.

"School ended a month after the prom. I was relentless in chasing after him that summer. We were married in September, and yes, it was a white wedding. I was a virgin."

Whoa, Michelle is a mind reader tonight—glad we didn't have to ask that awkward but necessary question!

"Preston was born a year to the day after the wedding. After him, I had three miscarriages, and I accepted that I couldn't have any more children. That became a sore subject between us, but it was only one of many. The man who was so sweet and gentle in the classroom was a tyrant at home. He would make weekly lists of daily chores I had to do, and I would get rewarded or punished accordingly. He controlled every aspect of my life. It was worse than living with my mother. We were both Catholic and divorce was out of the question. Besides, I was so young and insecure, I felt worthless and guilty since I was the one who had chased him. By the time Preston was in elementary school, I would go to church and pray to God to take me. I once crossed the highway with my eyes closed hoping to get hit. Instead, two months later, during a terrible storm, a tree fell on the road as Phillip drove home. It hit his car. He died instantly. I had a nervous breakdown, and went to confession twice a day, feeling guilty about the whole thing, although I never wished for *his* death. Anyway, I spent the next several years finishing my college degree, raising Preston, and, once a year, bringing flowers to my mother's and Phillip's graves. When Preston was in his last year of high school, we decided it would be a good time to move to the Southwest where the climate is warmer, taxes are lower, and I could be closer to Preston, who had been accepted by the University of Southern California.

"You know, when you're back East in these big, old cities, under gray skies and soiled snow, you have romantic images of the West; skies eternally blue, sprawling ranches with families growing their own vegetables, milking their own cows, kissing the tall, silent cowboy. You know what I mean. We came over on a brief vacation, spent our time at a dude ranch and went home with even more unrealistic fantasies than the ones we had started with.

"That's why I bought that big old house out in the boonies. God, how I ended up hating the place. With Preston gone to college, my only companions were scorpions and cockroaches. Well, we also had occasional coyotes. The good thing about that house, it kept me busy, because it needed constant repair. Still, I had too much time on my hands. That's when I decided to get my real-estate license, I figured that way I could control my own working hours. That was another nice fantasy.

"The day I got my license, I went out to celebrate with a few other newly anointed Realtors. We went to this karaoke bar, and after much prodding, I ended up on the stage, a microphone in my hands. I sang, "You Don't Bring Me Flowers." You remember that song? It was a duet with Barbra Streisand and Neil Diamond. Soon I had a little crowd cheering. Suddenly a man gets up on the stage, grabs another microphone and starts singing the Neil Diamond part. It was magic; we didn't miss a beat, and the crowd went wild. That's how I met John.

"It wasn't love at first sight. He was a recovering alcoholic, and we met at a bar. Not a good sign. Because of my mother I had vowed never to get involved with a man who drinks. Also, he wasn't Catholic. We dated for a year. He had been clean and sober for over ten years and he still went to monthly meetings. I went with him a few times and met some of the people he was mentoring, and heard the words of thanks and affection they expressed to him. When he converted to Catholicism I started to believe that maybe there was hope and love left for me.

Maybe I wouldn't have to go through the rest of my life alone. John's health wasn't the greatest; he was on disability and I was certainly the one with the money in our case. Our parish priest married us. Preston was happy for me, knowing I had someone in my life. I sold real estate; John worked on the house and ran errands. But mostly and more importantly, he loved me. I was always the most important part of his life, and he made me feel loved, cherished, and irreplaceable. I no longer felt like a big nothing.

"When his cancer returned, it all happened very quickly. We knew it was going to happen, but no matter what you read or are told, you're never ready for it—for the moment when you lose the love of your life. John had thought of everything down to when the doctors were to pull the plug and let him go. He knew me well because I could have never done that, never. Saying good-bye to him was the hardest thing I've ever done. John will forever be with me, in my heart, in my soul. He still guides me and comforts me. We will be together in the afterlife." Michelle's eyes were the only dry ones in the house. "I'm not telling you this so you'll feel sorry for me. I'm telling you this so you know that true, unconditional love is not a fantasy, and you never know when or where you may find it."

We dried our eyes, hugged each other, and decided to postpone Lisa's wedding plans to a later day. We all left with lighter steps and lighter hearts, for despite her loss, Michelle had experienced what we all dream of and sometimes think is just a fantasy—everlasting love.

Is It Tool Time Yet?

If you build it, will they come?

Love has many facets, as many as there are "objects of desire." We all know someone who would rather leave a mate than a pet, or a man more willing to loan his wife than his car. But Jenny's passion was a little more unusual—construction. Not papier-mâché or castles-in-the-air construction, no, I'm talking hammers and nails and whatever else construction people use to build houses. No wonder she was so popular among us single female boomers! You need to hang a picture straight? Call Jenny. Your sink is clogged on a holiday? Call Jenny. Your sprinkler system is acting crazy and watering the neighborhood hot tub late at night instead of your flowers in the morning? Call Jenny. Yes, we all had Jenny's number on speed dial. But there was more to Jenny than her love of power tools and construction paraphernalia. And in the end, it was through that passion that she landed her soul mate. Here is Jenny's story.

Jenny is a cute, size-2 petite, with all her original parts. She is very creative and has a professional portfolio to prove it. You see, Jenny worked as a product designer for a big company that manufactures and sells the kind of things aimed to separate tourists from their dollars. If you ever purchased a souvenir mug at an airport, or a T-shirt with a touristy slogan, chances are it was designed by Jenny. In general, her creations have a delicate look, an artistic combination of colors, and they always make you feel like you are buying something special. That's one more reason people are quite stunned to hear about her fascination with power tools and other gadgets we usually associate with strong, rough, manly hands.

We talked about that as we walked into the hardware store.

"Imagine that," Jenny said to me. "You'd think *tool* is a four-letter word."

"Hmmm, Jenny, actually, it is."

"Oh, don't be silly, you know what I mean, not that kind of four letters."

We paced up and down Home Depot's aisles. Jenny likes to do this when she is in a rut or having a bad day. Today I was with her because I needed lightbulbs.

"I must be getting old," she said.

"We all are. What brought that up? Don't get turned on by the sight of a sheet of plywood, anymore?"

"You haven't noticed?"

"Noticed what?"

"Nobody has offered to help me yet."

"Jenny, we're at Home Depot, not Neiman Marcus."

"Exactly. Normally I have people fighting to help me."

"People? You mean men," I said, while inspecting her micro-miniskirt and her small, hard nipples poking through her halter top. It was January and I wore sweats under my coat while Jenny, who, as far as I knew, wasn't experiencing hot flashes, was wearing next to nothing.

Just then, a man donning the store's trademark orange apron approached us and asked Jenny if she needed help. Since I was the only one there with the intention of purchasing something, I expected the man to address my needs. Wrong. I was obviously invisible. Jenny and the orange-apron guy quickly became engulfed in a discussion about windows, something about e-grade and heat transfer, and they walked toward the windows-and-doors department while I was left in the electrical aisle, clueless. At least the car keys were safely hidden in my purse. I dug out my reading glasses and the burned-out bulb and started checking and comparing. *I can do this, who needs a man? More important, who needs Jenny?* I kept telling myself, feeling more or less like poor orphan Annie.

By the time Jenny reappeared, I had found the lightbulbs, paid for them, looked at all the different sizes of flowerpots available, munched on a health bar, and drank a whole bottle of designer water. I was tempted to get in my car and leave her there, stranded, in her frost-bite outfit, but, since she was my best friend, I waited. She walked toward me, with this great big smile on her face, and she looked like someone who just swallowed a lightbulb, aglow!

"Okay Jenny, spit it out."

"What?" She could hardly conceal the twinkle of pleasure in her eyes.

"I bet you have a date."

Now she laughed openly as I unlocked the car's doors. "No, not really a date." She played coy with me—as if. "He's coming over after work to give me his opinion."

"His opinion on what? Your bra size?"

"Oh, you are so baaad!" Her voice trailed on the "a" and she giggled. "Besides, you know I'm not wearing a bra. No, I told him about the sunroom I would like to build by my kitchen—"

"How clever. So he comes over at night to talk about sunrooms. I get it; he'll have to spend the night so he can tell you where the sun hits in the early morning."

"Ha ha. You are so funny. Gordon isn't like that."

"Gordon? First-name basis already, are we? Look I don't want to rain on your parade, but I'm your friend and I know your habits. I'm not sure it is a good idea for a perfect stranger to visit you at night."

"Why don't I come in and change your lightbulb?" Jenny offered.

"Nope, I'm perfectly capable of changing my lightbulb. I'm driving you home, which should give you plenty of time to make up some sketches of your imaginary sunroom just in case this Gordon actually remembers to ask." And that's what I did. She got out of the car all giggly and happy. That's Jenny.

I was getting daily reports on Gordon's expertise and the amount of money Jenny spent on new power tools. When Jenny gets excited over words like "Husky" she is talking tools' brands, not men. In spite of my good intentions, I ended up asking her why. "Why are you spending all that money on tools? They end up hanging in your garage with the rest of them."

"I'm practicing."

"Practicing what? Wait, please don't tell me you are actually going through with the sunroom. As a friend I think it's insane. As a Realtor, I'm telling you it's nuts. You'll never get your money back and honestly, do we need a sunroom in the desert?"

"No sunroom." She lowered her voice as if sharing some hypnotic secret. "I'm preparing for my test."

That left me speechless. Jenny was taking a test? A test involving construction equipment? What was that about? I knew that somehow it all tied in with Gordon.

"I'm getting a contractor's license," Jenny said. "To prove I have enough hands-on hours, I help Gordon at his part-time remodeling job."

"Jenny, are you going to trade ink and pencils for hammering nails into people's walls?" I said, while intently staring at her slender hands and French-manicured fingernails.

"My dear, there is more to construction than hammering nails. Gordon and I are perfectly in sync when it comes to working, and we get along fine even after work." She said all that with such a solemn tone you would have thought she was reading from the Bible.

"Okay, I'll buy that. Any way I can get to see some of the work you two did? Just out of curiosity, you understand."

Jenny smiled.

The following Saturday I drove to the "work site" as Jenny called it. I recognized her car, and parked mine along the curb in front of this fabulous mansion. Jenny flung open the front door before I had a chance to ring the bell. She had on a modest T-shirt under a coverall and believe it or not, she actually wore a tool belt, just like the construction people I often saw in the builders' ads. Whoa! She looked so excited, pink cheeks, bright eyes and all. She took off her work gloves, grabbed my arm and pulled me behind her into the kitchen. Unlike the rest of the pristine house I'd walked through, the kitchen was a mess; nearly gutted, with electrical wires hanging from the ceiling. I recognized Gordon even without the orange apron. He stood by a makeshift tabletop and he had steaming coffee and doughnuts set out for us. I didn't have the heart to tell him I'd rather eat the box than the doughnuts. I smiled and joined in. Jenny and Gordon told me the owners were on vacation until next week so the remodeling had to be completed before they returned. I recognized Jenny's creative touch on the sketches on the stool and I complimented her on them. She corrected me: "Blueprints, they're called blueprints." Gordon shook his head and smiled.

Seeing the two of them together for the first time put a whole new perspective on their partnership. A month later, Jenny passed her test and became a bona fide building contractor. Just before Arizona's big construction boom, too. Jenny and Gordon quit their jobs and started a company together.

I see little of them as they are very busy, but Jenny offers to change my lightbulbs or repair my sprinklers any time I need her. She is still my best friend. Last week she called me from New Mexico and sounded so excited that I figured she'd gotten married or won the lottery. Nope, better than that, she said. She and Gordon bought a piece of dirt in the Land of Enchantment and are planning on building their dream home. Jenny is designing it, of course, and she promised me the guest room will be designed in my favorite colors. What can I say? Never underestimate the power of tools.

"To be successful, the first thing to do is fall in love with your work."—**Sister Mary Lauretta**

Flying the Friendly Skies

Lovers in and out of uniform.

I'm a real-estate agent so I meet a lot of people. That's how I became involved in the lives of the people whose story I'm about to tell. While the story describes the lives and relationships of more than one person, the perfect example of the horse-with-blinders type of lover is without doubt Sandra. I'm not saying that it's good or bad, I'm simply telling her story.

Tab called me first. He had a deep voice with a slight twang, though I couldn't place the regional accent. Tab said a flight attendant, one of my former clients, had given him my name. He wanted to purchase a house in Phoenix—something he could use between flights. He was tired of sharing a condo with six other pilots on alternate shifts, and since he liked to fix stuff, a house that needed some work would be perfect. We made an appointment to meet on his next layover and I began to preview properties.

For our first meeting, he showed up in a sleek silver Lexus with a sophisticated blonde sitting next to him. I could see his pilot's uniform hanging in the back of the car, and Tab explained that he was on call.

Sandra, the blonde, turned out to be very friendly. She explained that she was a flight attendant. Up close, Sandra looked old enough to be Tab's mother. A very well-preserved mother. Ten minutes into the meeting it became apparent they were a couple. He was driving her Lexus. We had three houses to look at. Every time Tab made a comment about the state of repairs of a property, he'd say something like: "My dad thinks . . ." Or, "My dad says . . ."

So, Tab was a daddy's boy. From Missouri. I would like to tell you that he was sexy, charming, sophisticated, and funny. He was none of those. He wasn't bad looking, and I'm sure he had his personable moments, but, more important, he was genuinely attracted to older women. Unfortunately, the other thing I came to learn about him over the months we spent searching for the perfect home was that he was a liar and a cheater and not very choosy when it came to older women.

If you assumed he was interested in Sandra's money (I did, at first) you'd be as wrong as I was. Sure he enjoyed the benefits her wealth brought, but he would have dated her even if she wasn't rich. I'm giving him some kudos for that.

Every time we went house shopping, I would meet Tab and Sandra at the first home and we'd go from there. We spent many hours together, and the more I got to know Sandra, the more I liked her. However, I just couldn't get past her infatuation with Tab. Sandra was originally from Seattle. She was a retired executive from Microsoft, and that explained part of her wealth. She inherited the rest.

"I met Tab on my first flight," Sandra said one day when we were having lunch in a small bistro in old-town Scottsdale. Tab would be gone several days; he was visiting his dad in between flights.

"How long ago was that?" I asked.

Sandra laughed softly. Her whole face lit up every time she spoke about Tab. "Last Christmas Eve," she said. "The airline always assigns the bad shifts to the newcomers, and it was my very first flight. I was sooo nervous. Tab must have seen it in my eyes. He did all he could to calm me down, even made me smile. By landing time we were friends, and we went out for drinks. By New Year we were lovers."

I counted mentally. This was April. Hmm . . . "What made you decide to be a flight attendant?" I stopped short of adding "at your age."

"I was bored, had done the volunteer route for too long. Oh, sheesh, who am I trying to fool? I'm crazy about uniforms, *men* in uniforms, I mean. The airline was hiring and they clearly stated that boomers were encouraged to apply, so I did. Never regretted it."

We sipped our wine in silence. This was our first nonprofessional outing. We were just two friends having lunch. At least I was.

"I . . ." Sandra hesitated.

I looked at her, puzzled.

"I need to leave town," she said.

"Overtime?" I joked.

"Surgery," she stated. "Elective surgery." That's girls' code for *plastic* surgery.

My eyes searched her face; she didn't look like she needed surgery, but hey, we all see ourselves differently in the mirror. I waited.

"I'll be flying to Kansas City in the morning," Sandra said. "It's a very involved procedure. I'm having a tummy tuck, and simultaneously they'll cut me all the way around, just above my belly button, and pull my skin up from my knees to my waist and down from under my breasts to meet at the waist." She must have noticed the look of sheer disbelief in my eyes because she patted my hand gently as she continued: "It's complicated, but this Kansas City surgeon is the best. He came highly recommended. He is pricey, but what's money for if not to help you be the best you can be?"

I still couldn't find my voice: ugly pictures of Sandra inside a colorful magician's box, being sawed in two, kept crowding my mind. I also lost my appetite.

"You see, I used to be very heavy. Then I went on a diet and lost over sixty pounds, but that left all that loose skin hanging. You don't notice when I'm dressed, but once the pantyhose are gone . . ."

I was getting the picture. Sandra was redesigning herself for Tab. "Tab knows?" I asked.

She shook her head. "He thinks I'm going to Seattle to take care of a sick friend. It's better that way."

Sandra expected my cooperation. I agreed.

She left the next day, and I didn't expect to hear from her or Tab for about a week.

The feminine voice on the phone sounded mysterious and sexy. She said her name was Lauren and that she was Tab's friend. Another one? I fought the urge to ask if she was a flight attendant and stuck strictly to business.

"What can I do for you?" I asked.

"I need to sell my house, and Tab highly recommended you." I sent a mental thanks to Tab.

"I may even buy another house; it depends." Her voice was definitely the kind advertisers like to use to coerce unsuspecting males into spending large amounts of cash for stuff only girls would love. Very sultry!

She gave me directions and that same afternoon I showed up at her house, loaded with information about her subdivision. Her home was cute in a girlish kind of way, too many pastels and ruffled curtains, too many silk plants, but we could fix all that.

I'm a woman and I'm straight, but I tell you, I couldn't keep my eyes off Lauren. Whoa! She was tall and thin, like a fashion model, dressed in a trampy, chic way that is hard to describe but certainly complemented her well. Add to that a flawless, creamy complexion; long wild, black hair; full red lips; and you forgot all of it the instant you saw her eyes. The eyes of a gypsy. My mind ran wild. I bet Bizet knew someone with those eyes when he wrote Carmen. And Lauren was Tab's *friend?* Tab from Missouri? No way.

Well, yes way. Lauren was a flight attendant, as you might have guessed. Same company as Sandra and Tab. I was beginning to feel like I was reading a forbidden diary. I couldn't wait to hear how well she knew Tab, and all this time I was trying to guess her age. I couldn't. She could have been anywhere between thirty-five and fifty. I soon found out that I was wrong. Lauren was fifty-two. When I told her she looked marvelous, she laughed, showing her perfect teeth. Darn, no fair. She helped me measure the rooms for the listing, and while going from room to room, I noticed photos of Lauren and Tab. The way they held on to each other left no doubts that they were lovers. I wondered if it was too late to track down Sandra and tell her to jump out of the magician's box, pronto. Then I remembered I was just the Realtor and no one was asking my opinion about love connections. Good. I felt less guilty listing the house. But driving back to the office, I couldn't help asking myself how to handle this situation, and what about Tab? He knew I was friends with Sandra.

So began the messy entanglement of the Realtor with a conscience, caught between gorgeous Lauren, who I figured knew nothing about Sandra, and lovely Sandra, who was risking her life to be more appealing to Tab the Cad.

By the time Sandra was back in Arizona, we had accepted an offer on Lauren's place, and, thank God, I hadn't heard from Tab. I wasn't sure I could keep my fingernails off his lying eyes. Maybe he changed his mind about buying a house. Maybe he was planning to move in with . . . whom? Sandra or Lauren? Well, Lauren's house was sold, so that would leave only Sandra with *her* palatial place. Good. No, nothing was good about this, but I didn't know what to do to help.

I went to visit Sandra, and she was walking and laughing. She looked so happy!

"I'll be able to be back to work in no time," Sandra said. "I do miss work and all the camaraderie." Not to mention Tab the Cad. I had trouble focusing. Poor Sandra.

"I heard you met Lauren." Had I not been sitting down I would have fallen off my platform shoes, I swear. I did choke on the air I was breathing, and Sandra slapped my back hard. That gave me enough time to come up with a clever answer.

"Lauren? Oh, yeah, Lauren." Mm hmm. Very clever.

"Tab told me. It's not a secret. He loves me, of course, but he's being pressured by his dad. You know how that goes. Tab's an only child. His folks want grandkids. I can't give him that, and Lauren can."

What did she just say? Lauren can? Fifty-two-year-old Lauren? She'd told me she had a hysterectomy ten years ago! My mind was screaming, *Sandra, wake up!* This was a bad situation, and like it or not, I was caught in the middle. I needed to talk to somebody, so I went to my broker—my boss, in real estate lingo. He was sympathetic *and* very forceful in making me promise that I'd stay out of it. He said that I was involved with the three of them in a professional relationship, and that did not include what people do under the covers behind closed doors.

That night I couldn't sleep: I wished a lot of bad luck to Tab. I know, it's bad karma and all that; I just couldn't help myself. So, Sandra knew about Lauren, but Lauren never mentioned Sandra. Hmm!

A week into escrow with Lauren's place, she decided she wanted to buy a house in Phoenix after all. That meant more professional time spent together, more commission for me, and I owed more thanks to Tab. I sat with Lauren and asked her to describe her dream home so that I could start searching. The most important item on her list was privacy; she wanted a home in a very secluded area, hard to find. Maybe she wanted to hide from Tab? No such luck. I noticed a deep sadness in her beautiful eyes as she spoke of "hard to find" and commented that it was an unusual request. That's when Lauren told me her secret.

"I have a son," she said. "He is barely over eighteen and has been in and out of trouble for the last three years. Trouble with the law. Drugs. Drugs and other bad things." Her eyes had turned a darker shade of brown and the sparkle was gone. No, it was more than just the sparkle, it was as if someone had turned off the lights. Grief slipped from her eyes and spread. I actually had goose bumps covering my arms.

"He always finds me," she said, her voice barely audible. "I keep moving." She glanced at me and saw the horrified look on my face before I could mask it. She said, "You think I'm a bad mother, don't you?"

They don't teach you about these things in real-estate school, and she was right, I did think she was a terrible mother.

"Tough love," she said. "It's a support group; it helps. They teach you to be strong. I have to. He broke probation again. I'm not strong. If he finds me I can't send him away. So I keep moving. Will you help me?"

I nodded because the knot in my throat didn't let me speak. Where did Tab fit in this picture? I wasn't about to ask. It turned out I didn't need to.

"Tab doesn't understand," she said, "about my son. He wants me to let him find me and then call the cops. I could never do that to my child. Perhaps if there was a strong male figure in my son's life . . ." Tab the Cad? A father figure? What a joke. I kept reminding myself I was there to sell real estate, but boy, was this getting complicated. Now I felt sorry for Lauren and for Sandra, and for myself.

We found the house and that evening decided to go out for pizza. Lauren and I met around happy hour, though she wasn't drinking because she was flying out that same evening. We had sat down and ordered when Tab came through the door with a group of pilots and flight attendants still in uniforms. They had just landed. Tab spotted us and quickly assembled more chairs in our corner, and everybody joined us and ordered beer and pizza. They were happy and loud and talking about men, women, who was sleeping with whom, that kind of stuff. I kept quiet, as I knew only Lauren and Tab.

Then Tab started to talk about this woman he used to date. He was giving private details but no names. He said he decided to break it off when she had this bizarre operation. With ample gestures he showed where this woman had been cut and how her skin had been pulled tight.

"It was like having sex with Frankenstein's monster, like a body assembled from different parts. I was afraid the screws would fall off and she'd come apart." He slapped his thigh and laughed out loud. Most of the men joined in. The women laughed too, but without much conviction. He had just given a cruel description of Sandra's surgery. I had no way of knowing if anyone else at the table knew about it. I couldn't stand it. I excused myself, put some money on the table, and left.

On my way home I called Sandra on my cell. She was on her way to the airport to substitute for someone who called in sick. I found enough courage to ask if she had broken up with Tab. "No, of course not, we were in Seattle together just last weekend, and we had a marvelous time. Why do you ask?"

"I don't know," I lied. "I haven't seen him around for a while, just curious."

"Thanks for caring. Rest assured, all is well in paradise."

Yeah, paradise all right. Staying out of the mess was getting harder and harder. I did close on the new house for Lauren and carefully avoided Tab—commission or not, I couldn't stand the sight of him. And I couldn't help wondering how many older women he was seeing.

Then it happened. Against all odds, Sandra and Lauren ended up working the same flight. I don't know where Tab was, but it doesn't matter. It was a flight from Los Angeles to Maui. They spent the night there in adjoining rooms. Now remember, Lauren knew nothing about Sandra, and although Sandra knew of Lauren, she had been told lies about her and had never actually met her. They left the door between the rooms open and chatted while changing for dinner. Lauren noticed the scars on Sandra's body; they had healed well but were still quite noticeable. She kindly inquired, wondering if they were due to female troubles. Trying to make Sandra feel less self-conscious, Lauren volunteered that she too had had female problems and had to have a hysterectomy years ago.

They had not made the Tab connection yet. Sandra, always open and friendly, explained that it was elective surgery. "To please my younger lover," she said, and then went on describing the procedure. Something finally clicked in Lauren's head. She quietly asked if Sandra was still dating the younger man. Sandra proudly showed Lauren her new friendship ring; Lauren slowly lifted her hand and put her finger next to Sandra's. They were wearing matching rings. After a long silence, they looked at each other and said: "Tab!"

The tough-love support group came through for Lauren; she broke up with Tab, left the flight-attendant job, and went back to teaching. Unfortunately, Sandra wasn't so tough. Last I saw her, she was still waiting for Tab to ask her to marry him. She no longer talks to me. I'm not sure why, except that maybe she felt betrayed because I knew the truth about Lauren. I've long since made peace with the decisions I made and the things I did and didn't do as an unwilling fourth in their ménage à trois.

About a month ago I answered my cell phone and heard the unmistakable Missouri twang coming through loud and clear. Tab the Cad had the nerve to ask me out. Me? Why? I wasn't a flight attendant. I wasn't beautiful like Lauren, or charming and forgiving like Sandra. The only thing I had in common with them was, well, hey, I *am* older. But not dumb. I hung up the phone and laughed all the way to the office.

Happily Ever After

You will see it when you believe it.

In a world prone to split everything and everyone, it is nice to know that some people beat the odds and find true love. Judy didn't find true love early in life. I was a bridesmaid at her wedding. Sadly I wasn't there a few years later, at divorce time. By then I had moved to Arizona. We reconnected one Christmas season when she visited the Valley and have stayed in touch ever since. Here is Judy's story.

"Why do they call them love handles? What's there to love? I wish I could just—" Jessica made a motion as if clipping her skin with imaginary scissors.

"Don't pull on the skin," Judy said. "For God's sake, Jessica, it looks like that because skin loses elasticity after a certain age. By pulling on it, you're not helping. It's sort of like the elastic on your underwear, once it starts to go, you can't—"

"Okay, I got it. That's going to be the next thing to go."

Judy turned her head so Jessica couldn't see her giggling. Jessica lay on her bedroom carpet, wiggling and huffing, trying to zip up the skintight jeans she'd just bought. Not any jeans, Jessica would say, *designer* jeans! She claimed they had shrunk in the dryer, but Judy knew better. Judy and Jessica had been friends for a long time, and while they were both the same age, Jessica looked at least ten years younger. It wasn't because of healthy living; it was because of the good plastic surgeon she visited often.

The zipper now secured, Jessica readjusted her double-D implants into her La Perla bra and went back into her ballroom-size closet to find the appropriate top. To Judy, Jessica's closet was like the ones you see in the movies. Several of the racks were on tracks; push a button and voilà, the clothes started moving, just like the ones at the dry cleaner's. At first it was amusing, but after watching the carousel of clothing go round and round, Judy started feeling nauseated. So, she decided to wait in the bedroom while Jessica tried on top after top.

It was getting late. The appointment was for three o'clock, and the place was about ten minutes from Jessica's house. That gave them five minutes.

"Jessica, let's go. Why are you getting all dressed up? We're going there and back, aren't we?" She glanced inside her purse to make sure her $100-discount coupon was in there. "I'm still feeling funny about all this, you know. The idea of having live botulism injected into my forehead—I don't know."

"Stop analyzing everything. Thousands of people do it daily—younger people. You owe it to yourself. You're in your prime, about to retire and move to Arizona. You're healthy, single—what are you waiting for?"

As Judy opened her mouth to disagree, her eye caught a flash of color? "Jessica, is that a tattoo?"

"Oh, yes. Like it?" Jessica pulled up her top to show the small of her back. There was this little cute heart with two letters underneath: BC.

"BC? What does it stands for? Before Christ?"

Jessica laughed out loud, "No, silly, it's for Bike Chick."

"Bike Chick? You don't have a bike, do you?"

"Judy, Judy," she chided, "I don't have a bike, but the men I date do, most of them at least. Let's go get your Botox, so you can thank me later."

Jessica insisted on driving her Mercedes. Everything Jessica did was aimed at impressing people. Judy and Jessica met years before at a driving school, both taking a class to make up for a speeding ticket. Back then, Judy was a young professor of English literature at a small community college. Jessica worked as a private secretary. Soon after they met, their lives took a strange turn. Jessica married her boss, who left his wife of thirty years for her. Judy's husband decided he wanted to live in solitude and write the next Great American Novel, so he left her without so much as a note.

While Jessica was on an extended honeymoon at an undisclosed exotic place, Judy had a nervous breakdown and ended up in a medical facility. It was there she'd first met Benito. Benito was a political refugee from Central America. It was hard to tell his age. The man was short and stocky, with long, black hair woven in a single braid, which hung down to his waist. He wore a gold loop on his left earlobe. Back then, it was quite an unusual sight. He worked as a nurse's aide on the night shift. He hardly spoke, but when he did, it was with a strong, funny accent and Judy had trouble understanding him.

Benito spent a lot of time fussing over Judy and she assumed it was because of her looks. Not that she was beautiful or glamorous, but her complexion was very light, her hair naturally blond, and when she stood next to him she was a good four inches taller—even in her hospital slippers. Late one evening, when she couldn't sleep, they sat and talked mostly about how much he missed his small village and his family. Judy spoke of her work. He was fascinated and treated her like a Nobel Prize winner. That's how Judy and Benito became friends: two lonely people and many sleepless nights. Judy made it her mission to help Benito improve his English skills. When the time came for her to go back into the world, Judy gave Benito her phone number and her address and asked him to stop by some weekend when he wasn't working.

The slamming of brakes (Jessica's way of parking) brought Judy back to reality.

"Here we are, Tootsie." Jessica called Judy "Tootsie" because she thought it sounded more glamorous. But Judy wasn't exactly *feeling* glamorous. She only agreed to the Botox experience because she'd received a $100-off coupon in the mail and because she was curious about this miracle injection that could make your wrinkles disappear.

"You're sure it doesn't hurt?" Judy asked for the hundredth time.

"Promise. It's just a little prick. Now, I haven't been to this place before, but let's see what they have to offer."

The office was small, with large windows looking onto a sunny courtyard. Everything was decorated in purple. The wait was short, and Jessica insisted on going into the room with Judy to watch. The doctor, a young woman, must have answered all of Jessica's questions correctly because Jessica decided to get a treatment herself, some injections for her lips to plump them up. Jessica was right about the Botox: it was a little prick, didn't hurt, and didn't make her feel any different. The doctor said it would be about a week before she would see the results. While waiting for Jessica to get her injection, Judy kept looking at her forehead in the various mirrors, half expecting her wrinkles to disappear before her eyes. Whatever Jessica was getting done to her lips must have been painful—she could tell just by the expression on her face, and Jessica was usually a pro at that stuff. When they left, Jessica suggested they stop for a drink or maybe a matinee.

Jessica had been single for two years now. Her husband had left her for his latest secretary; a buxom blonde in her mid twenties. It was history repeating itself. Jessica got to keep the house and a generous alimony, which she spent freely in the pursuit of youth and happiness. She dated men fast and furiously, as if her love life had an expiration date.

While they were walking, Judy asked, "Are you seeing anyone?"

"Am I seeing anyone?" Jessica said. "Of course I am. Life is short and getting shorter. I'm talking to a man from, get this, Albuquerque. I may fly out there next weekend. So, Tootsie, will you be leaving our sunny California for a mound of sandy desert?"

"I don't know, I can't make up my mind. It would be a good decision money-wise, but it would be like starting over—new surroundings, new lifestyle, and new friends. I guess I'm not sure I want to leave my friends. After all, they are my family."

"Anyone in particular?" Jessica chided.

Judy knew Jessica was hinting at Benito, but she decided she wasn't going to get into that argument again. "Oh, Jessica, you know you are like a sister to me. So, are we going to catch a movie?" The choice of a suitable movie was enough to distract Jessica from the "Benito" subject, at least for now.

After the movie, they went back to Jessica's place, and Judy got into her Toyota and left. Jessica was right about one thing: she needed to decide. She still lived in the same two-bedroom duplex she bought when she'd been married. She could sell that and buy a nice place in Arizona, in one of those gated communities for people over fifty with golf courses, pools, and other interesting, activities. But what about Benito? If someone was family, it was certainly he. They had been together over ten years now.

She remembered that first time he showed up at her place. A month or so after she had resumed her regular life, he was at her front door, without calling first. He'd brought her a book about his country, in English. They'd sat on the patio, drinking tea, and he pointed to pictures of places familiar to him, places he would probably never see again in his lifetime. His voice had been sad, a deeply touching kind of sadness, the one you don't speak of, the one that's always with you. On impulse, she'd offered to continue helping him with his English on weekends. In exchange, he offered to take care of her Post-it–size yard. And so it began. He would show up on Saturday morning, work in the yard, which was now a lush, scented oasis, read with Judy in the afternoon and then they would take turns cooking and eating by candlelight. It was fun and Benito would stay longer and longer until one Saturday evening, he didn't leave at all. Judy was well aware of the culture and income difference, but somehow it didn't matter. When Benito was with her it was as if a cloak of serenity protected her from the outside world. She grew accustomed to his presence; he would do little things for her, like picking up her dry cleaning and leaving it on her patio, fixing the garbage disposal, even scrubbing her saltillo floors on his knees when she wanted to remove the old coating. But most important, he was a perfect lover, attentive and romantic.

With Benito in her life, the memories of her former husband began to fade. All was perfect and wonderful until they started to go out in public together. The reaction from her friends was astonishing; they treated Benito as some strawberry picker on the run from the law. After five years, Benito had become a U.S. citizen and soon after that, he completed his classes and was now a respiratory therapist. But to all her friends he was still the illegal with the Cochise hairdo. He moved in permanently after he received his first raise and could contribute his share to the household's expenses. Pride was a big part of Benito's character. Their life together may have appeared dull to outsiders, but it was perfect to them. Once when the subject of marriage had come up, Judy was vocal about not wanting to be remarried and Benito never spoke of it again.

The morning after the Botox event, Judy was awakened by the chime from her cell phone. She grabbed it quickly, not wanting to wake Benito. "Hi, Jessica," she whispered. "What's up?" The sound coming from the mouthpiece was garbled; she knew the caller was Jessica because she recognized the number. "Are you all right?"

"Nnn—no—no."

"I'll be right over." Judy grabbed her jeans and a T-shirt, brushed her teeth, and out the door she went, but not before kissing Benito lightly on the forehead as he slept. Jessica's front door was wide open, and Jessica was waiting, a silk scarf covering her head and part of her face and dark glasses. She held a fistful of tissues over the lower part of her face. She moved her hand before Judy had a chance to talk. "Oh, my God! Jessica, what happened? Did someone beat you up?"

Jessica shook her head in denial.

"Your lips, your face." She looked like those faces you see pressed against a glass pane, the red, swollen lips taking over most of the face. "You think it was that injection, that thing, yesterday?"

Jessica nodded yes, tears sliding from under the dark glasses, landing on the wad of tissues.

"Let's go, I'll take you to the emergency room. Do you need anything? Get in my car, I'll lock up your house. Do you have your keys? Let's go."

Hours later, with Jessica resting comfortably in her own bed, Judy called home to let Benito know what was going on. Jessica was so pumped full of anti this and anti that, that she'd probably sleep though the day. And Judy couldn't help reflecting on how Jessica—with all her money, all her beauty, and all her beaus—ended up calling her, Judy, in times of need. What would happen if she moved to Arizona?

On the flip side of the coin, Judy had Benito, always there, always dependable. Dependable wasn't a good choice of words, she thought. Benito was a lot more than that. She remembered that bad winter, a few years back when she'd been so ill. Every little noise, every bit of light, had made her nauseated and Benito, her Benito, hung dark sheets over each window in the house, and used blankets and towels to muffle every outside noise and never left her bedside.

He didn't need to tell her he loved her; he *was* love in the purest form. After all these years together, Judy realized for the first time the deep, emotional connection between them. Benito was more than her lover, he was her soul mate. She couldn't wait to get home and kiss his face and hold him tight. Poor Jessica would never experience this kind of high, this kind of fusion, Judy thought.

By the time the sun went down, Jessica was finally coming out of it. Judy left plenty of ice water within reach, placed the remote on the night table, made sure the phone was working, and then left. When she arrived home, she was surprised to find the house dark—Benito should have been home by now. Maybe he stopped to grab some takeout on his way home. Finally she heard the garage door open. Judy hesitated for a minute. Should she run and hug him? He'd probably think she was crazy. She turned on all the lights as she walked toward the door leading to the garage, and there he was.

She stopped cold.

He was Benito all right, but a different Benito. His long braid was gone and his hair fell softly around his face, barely covering his earlobes. The gold hoop in his left lobe shined under the light. The cut showed silver streaks in his hair, and softened his nose line. He looked like a different man, a man of substance, a distinguished gentleman.

What a difference a haircut makes, she thought, but she still hadn't moved or spoken.

Benito's eyes searched for hers. "Say something," he said, in a gentle voice, with the sweetest accent. "It will grow back if you don't like it."

"I love it. No, I love you, all of you."

"Judy? Are you okay?"

"Never been better, but what possessed you to cut your hair?"

"I had to let go, it was the last reminder of my country. I'm a U.S. citizen, all I ever wanted is right here, right now."

"I'm glad to hear that because I have a very important question to ask you. . . . Would you marry me?"

Benito's face froze. He stepped back and looked at her, and she could tell he didn't quite know what to make of it. "Is that the way they do it here? The woman proposes? How nice. Wait, do you also get down on your knees and all that?" He said it laughing, a laugh full of joy and happiness. They kissed like they had never kissed before; Judy ran her fingers through the softness of his hair and mentally thanked Jessica and her obsession with the fleeting importance of looks for her newly found wisdom of the heart.

"If one is lucky, a solitary fantasy can totally transform one million realities."—Maya Angelou

Breakfast at Tiffany's

How to teach an old lover a new trick.

I met Holly when her husband, Al, died. I was friends with her neighbor, who suggested I talk to Holly in case she decided to sell her house. Although we were about the same age, since Holly had such a maternal attitude about her, I always felt as if she was older. Everybody in the neighborhood loved her to the point that they brought her their first produce from their gardens, and neighbors often gathered in her front yard. Holly made herself available for babysitting or pet walking, and her home always smelled of freshly baked goods. I thought she would have made a wonderful grandmother but since she never had children, she made a great owner to her pets. I was there from the beginning of the Holly-Frank romance. However, Tiffany, who lived with Holly, had a front-row seat in their relationship, and tells the story with more flair.

Okay, I'm sensitive, I admit it, but *anyone* can tell when Holly is upset. All you have to do is perk up your ears and the clattering sounds in the kitchen say it all.

I'm sitting quietly in the large chair by the sunniest window in the living room, while Holly is making tea. By the noise level in the kitchen, you'd think Holly is hand forging the teakettle. Shhh, here she comes, I better look happy. Uh oh, I don't see any tea—

"What are you looking at?"

Whoa, she is angry all right!

"He's gone forever, I'm sure." Holly wrings a pink tissue between her fingers and dabs her cheeks. I'm careful not to move—I sit and look up at her with the most sympathetic glance I can muster.

"I knew it, I just knew it," Holly goes on. "It was too good to last, these perfect years, all down the toilet, and why? Because of my love for my little darlings." She is looking at me again. I'm not sure how she expects me to respond, so I keep the I-feel-your-pain look going but I can tell what's coming next.

"Frank is the love of my life, always was, always will be."

Oh, no Holly, not the Frank story again.

"Tiffany, do you remember when Frank and I met? No, of course you don't. You weren't around then. I was working at the animal shelter, fresh out of high school. Frank was saving money for college. I was there because I love animals, cats in particular.

"Out of the blue he gets drafted, he said. I have my suspicions; I think his mother didn't like me, so he probably volunteered to avoid a confrontation. Anyway, before I can convince him to get married, he is gone, shipped to Vietnam. I write to him but he doesn't write back. I tried to stay in touch through his mother, but she had a knack for avoiding me. I figured she just wanted Frank for herself. So I waited patiently for his return." Holly stops and sighs.

I sit there and listen to the story I've heard before, what, a dozen times?

"A few years pass and one day, I'm at the drugstore picking up cat litter and who should come through the revolving doors but Frank, *my* Frank. I dropped everything and ran into his arms. Tiffany, you should have seen the surprise on his handsome face! Tears of joy streamed down my cheeks when I suddenly realized—he wasn't hugging me back! He was pushing me away? Hey! That's when from the corner of my eyes I saw them—his mother and a pregnant young woman.

"When Frank introduced me to his Vietnamese wife, he spoke like he had a frog in his throat. *I hope you choke,* I thought, but I didn't really mean it. I sprinted out of the store without shaking hands and even forgot the cat litter. That should tell you how upset I was. So upset that I packed my stuff, bought a new cat carrier and left town, headed straight for Phoenix, Arizona." Holly pauses and waits for my reaction.

I look at her with great love and concern in my blue eyes, and after a short hesitation, she goes back to her storytelling.

"I was lucky. In Phoenix I met Al, a nice man, a little older than me. We married and moved into a comfortable home on a large lot, with horse privileges. We could have had horses right there, in our backyard, if we wanted. We had dogs and cats instead. I tried chickens, but they were always sick, and I could never bring myself to kill them. After the last one died of natural causes, we gave that up."

That's the way Holly is, always looking out for pets and people.

"Al had two grown kids, and he had been fixed after the second one was born so we never had little ones. But I had my pets, and that was enough. Still, at times I would think about Frank and wonder where he was. Was he happy? Did he remember me? And sadness would overcome me.

"When Al passed away quietly in his sleep, I felt so lonely. Months went by. His life insurance paid off the house, and then his kids came and helped themselves to his stuff. I couldn't have cared less. I spent most of my time in bed, feeling victimized. First Frank and now Al. Was I destined to spend the rest of my life alone?

"Thank God for my pets. They had to be fed and kept clean and they became my reason for living." Holly grabs more tissues and blows her nose. She looks tired; she needs some sleep.

Before I can make a sound, she starts her story again. "At one point, I pined for Frank so bad, I tried to track him down through the Internet. I came to my senses before I spent too much money on that project. I figured I should get involved with some kind of volunteer organization to occupy my time, but I kept putting that off.

"Then one day I saw an ad in the local paper. The airport was hiring. They needed more personnel with all the new people moving to Phoenix. I thought, *What the heck, let's try.* They hired me! I went to work for one of the airlines with headquarters here in Phoenix, and although the pay wasn't much, I could fly free anywhere they went. Plus, I got to wear a really cute uniform. I worked three days a week and spent my off time reading up about all the locations I could travel to, soon, very soon. It was a little over a year since Al had passed away, and my life was getting very boring again. I kept dreaming about all the traveling I was going to do. I would talk to my pets about it, but then I never went anywhere.

"One afternoon toward the end of my shift, I went over to talk to Rita; she was one of the security people that X-rays your luggage and stuff. She was going to lend me a book about Hawaii. She had traveled there twice and told me it would be perfect for my first trip: I wouldn't need a passport, everybody speaks English, and it's a safe place for a single woman. The security checkpoint was unusually busy, so I figured I'd wait until Rita's break. She was operating the machine with the screen like a TV where you can actually see inside people's luggage. I always enjoyed hearing her stories about some of the unusual contents found in people's carry-ons. I stood against one of the big windows facing the runway, sipped my soda, and let the afternoon sun warm me through the large glass panes.

"With my mind wandering, I wasn't too attentive to Rita's screening process. Everything moved quickly and smoothly until some traveler kept setting off the alarm on the metal detector. Finally the officer just decided to run the wand up and down the man's body. Rita winked at me, motioning to the guy."

Holly closes her eyes, as if replaying the image in her head, and she smiles, a brief, mysterious smile. "He had his back to me, but he appeared to be middle-aged and in good shape. He raised his arms sideways to allow the security man to run the wand. Then he turned around as he was being patted down. That's when I dropped my paper cup; lid and all hit the floor. The man being patted down spun around to look. Our eyes met and while I was nervously wiping my skirt where drops of soda had landed, Frank let out a loud, 'Holly, is that you?'

"*Is that me? Duh!* He walked away from the inspection point, and gave me a bear hug. He held me so tight I couldn't breathe, and I was okay with that. I would have gladly run the risk of suffocation for such a warm embrace. We didn't hear the security man calling out, 'Sir, sir, you need to get your briefcase and your shoes.' Only then did I realize that Frank was in his socks. We happened to look at his feet together and when we looked up we both laughed—I'm not sure why.

"The rest of the encounter is pretty fuzzy. Thanks to my uniform, I was able to walk and chat with him all the way to his gate. I could tell he didn't want to get on that plane. He gave me his cell number and said he would call me as soon as he landed in San Francisco. In all the excitement, I forgot to ask about his wife."

This time there is no smile on Holly's face, only doubt. "Okay, that's not exactly true, I actually had to fight myself to keep from asking. I totally forgot about Rita's book on Hawaii and went straight home to my pets. Sure enough, Frank called. He called that evening and every evening after that. He had a job offer in Phoenix and when we bumped into each other he had just left the company after his second interview.

"'Holly, I need to decide,' he said. 'My wife is in Saigon visiting her family and our son is at boot camp. I'm alone here and Thuy, my wife, already told me she isn't moving to Phoenix. It's a great opportunity, I'm close to retiring and San Francisco isn't where I want to grow old.'

"What was I supposed to do? Frank is the love of my life. I told him to take the job and come stay with me. Tiffany, stop looking at me like that. He was my man before he went to Vietnam, remember?"

I do remember when Frank moved in with Holly. Everybody in the neighborhood knew about it because that was all she could talk about. Frank here, Frank there. By the time he arrived we expected him to walk on water. Six months later, Frank was a single man, left almost penniless by a hurried divorce, but he did look happy. Of course, there were some problems, or as I liked to call them, "adjusting pains," which probably come with every budding relationship. I don't know for sure as I've never been lucky or unlucky enough to be in one.

Almost right after the divorce, Frank began to talk about moving closer to the city; the large lot was too much maintenance and he wanted to spend more "quality time" with Holly—sort of making up for lost years. Yep, he knew exactly what to say, I tell you. But Holly was so in love she would have jumped into the canal if he asked. He didn't. He only wanted to move into a fancier house, in a fancier neighborhood, without the pets. Holly's pets. And that was the other problem.

The name was Buddy; he was originally Al's dog. By the time Al passed away, Buddy was old and grouchier than ever, and he wasn't crazy about sharing Holly's attention with Frank. It got a lot worse after the naked attack incident. Buddy was lucky Frank didn't shoot him dead on the spot. Well, I guess it's hard to carry a gun when you are naked.

Here is what happened: Buddy had slept in the master bedroom ever since he was a puppy and continued sleeping there after Frank moved in. Holly didn't have the heart to chase him out. Every time Frank and Holly made love, Buddy would growl and try to get between them. Frank finally put his foot down: Buddy had to sleep somewhere else. Holly installed one of those pet gates on the bedroom door so Buddy could sleep just outside and while he may growl, he wasn't going to jump on the bed. That seemed to appease Frank.

Frank's business required traveling and on this particular instance, he'd been out of town for about a week. His return flight was late and by the time he drove himself back home, it was the middle of the night. He took off his clothes in the living room as not to wake Holly, got into bed and completely forgot about Buddy and the gate. The minute Frank got under the covers, Holly started her little hand tricks. Soon, they were having some pretty intense sex, so intense that Holly howled in pleasure. Buddy jumped on the bed and pulled off the covers. He was snapping his teeth only inches from Frank's bare butt.

The poor man ended up naked against the wall while Holly dialed 911. She did come to her senses, restrained the dog and canceled the 911 call, but their sex life changed forever and we all knew Buddy had to go.

After that, Holly put her house up for sale and they decided to purchase a patio home. The new homeowners association allowed only two pets, but Holly's menagerie consisted of four. They had three months to decide which pets would stay and which would go. Holly arranged to go with Frank on his next trip, sort of a peace offering. It was only a three-day trip, so she paid a neighbor's teenager to take care of her pets.

Unfortunately, the pet sitter didn't lock the side gate properly after the evening feeding, and the dogs got out. They all had tags, and when Holly and Frank came back, they found them at the shelter. That was the good news. The bad news was that Buddy had been hit by a car and wasn't doing well. In the end, the vet recommended he be put down. That was a major tragedy with supersized guilt and unfortunate accusations flying around. We weren't sure the Frank-Holly romance was going to survive that spurt of ugliness. Although we all were very sorry for what happened to Buddy, we were also aware it was just one of those things that no one could foresee, including myself. And I'm pretty good at "sensing."

Poor Frank left on another business trip, without asking Holly to join him. I can't say I blamed him. He needed some time to think things out, I'm sure.

We're now on the fourth day of his absence. He hasn't called. And it appears Holly doesn't know where he's gone. The house feels pretty empty—first Buddy, now Frank. Who would leave us next? Holly has red-rimmed eyes and Cher's "If I Could Turn Back Time" is being played ad nauseam. Holly has been rummaging through Frank's desk and all his drawers looking for his passport. In her gloomy mood, she has visions of him flying to Saigon to reunite with the ex. On the seventh day—yes I know what you're thinking, but we are talking Frank, not God—I hear a loud knock at the door. Holly drags herself out of bed mumbling and sighing. On the doorstep stands Frank, her Frank, freshly shaved and wearing neatly pressed trousers and a white shirt. Holly appears stunned; she keeps opening and closing her mouth like a fish flirting with bait. I quickly slick down my hair, but no one is paying any attention to me anyhow.

Frank throws his arms around Holly, lifts her up, and says, "Good morning, sunshine. How about some breakfast?"

I'm not sure what her answer is, possibly something to the effect that she is in her pajamas and Frank is still holding her up. Instead of putting her down, he sweeps her up and carries her outside. Parked in the driveway is a huge motor home, just like the ones rock stars use for their concert tours. It is light gray, with windows and awnings, and it even has a name painted in large blue letters: CAT'S MEOW. I have to hand it to Frank, the man has style and a wicked sense of humor.

"Now we can travel together," says Frank, "and we can take our pets with us and as soon as I retire we can travel all over the United States and never be separated again, ever."

There are tears, of joy of course, and hugs and kisses, and many apologies. Frank cooks breakfast in the small kitchen. I am also hungry and I finally let them know, loudly.

"Poor Tiffany," says Holly running her fingers through my thick fur. "My poor little kitty. We need to get you some special food to celebrate."

I guess that means I'll be traveling with them. Hurray! What a relief. I need to do something special to show my appreciation. I know, I can work on those awnings. Better go sharpen my claws.

The Magic of Love

How much is that car in the window?

By the time we met, Alice was in her fifties. A devoted Catholic, she had given birth to five wonderful children, now grown and on their own. After being married for twenty-five years to her high school sweetheart, they divorced. There was a twinkle in her pale blue eyes when she told me the reason for the divorce: incompatibility. They had separated on good terms and still saw each other occasionally at family functions. He had married again, and again. Alice had remained single.

Alice lived in a storybook house on top of a cliff, with a great view of the Pacific. Her home was a sanctuary of serenity with the inland side of the grounds covered by mature, exotic plants that were home to birds and butterflies. At night, the crashing waves below were Alice's lullaby. She was a friend of the arts—once a week, she would open the fancy double doors of the house to local artists who came to mingle and share ideas and dreams.

From a distance, Alice's life was picture-perfect: She had children who loved her, plenty of friends, a constant flow of money from wise investments, a beautiful home, and every year a new Mercedes. But Alice had breast cancer.

Because she experienced a multitude of minor health problems, she had become very good about following preventative routines, among them, her monthly breast exam. On this particular day, her fingers felt the tiny knot on her left breast; ten minutes later she was on the phone with her doctor. In less than a week, she had a biopsy done. It was malignant, and soon Alice was undergoing the agony of chemotherapy. The story could end here, noting that the results were excellent and everyone hoped for Alice's quick recovery. But this is not the end of her story. This is where Alice's life changed forever—it was because of the cancer, or, in Alice's own words, "Thanks to my cancer."

This story is not about the power of positive thinking, although there is a lot of that in here. This is a story about the magic of love.

After the surgery to remove the nodule, Alice couldn't settle back into her everyday life. Her children wanted her to hire live-in help, but the idea didn't appeal to Alice. She asked her good friend Bob to move in. Bob was a gay man from the art community and would often act as her escort to social functions and other events. Because Bob lived modestly in a tiny studio with a view, he was elated to move into Alice's home, steps from the beach. The house was large enough so that they each had plenty of private space. In exchange, Bob would drive Alice to and from the chemotherapy sessions and keep things running smoothly and as close to normal as possible. This gave Alice's family peace of mind and allowed Alice a sense of independence while undergoing therapy. The arrangement was a great success; Bob and Alice got along fine—more than fine—they had a lot in common and enjoyed each other's company.

Bob gradually started noticing changes in Alice. By the second month of chemo, it became obvious that Alice handled her treatments more like a social event than a dreaded necessity.

She would dress in elegant, expensive outfits. Once her hair began to fall out, she practiced tying silk scarves in elaborate fashions over her bald head. No wigs for her!

Bob would drive her to the medical building, park the car, and take the elevator to the second floor. He made sure she was comfortably seated in the waiting room, and then went to wait for her at the coffee shop. She would have the staff call him on his cell when she was ready to be picked up. And instead of being feeble and tired, she would walk out of therapy peppy and smiling. The smile would usually last until the car left the parking lot. Then she would lay her head against the back of the seat and close her eyes. She never complained, but sometimes late at night Bob would hear her throwing up in the bathroom. Finally the last day of chemotherapy arrived. By then they had decided that the arrangement was working so well, Bob would stay at her house indefinitely. "Well, here we are, your last visit, Alice. I bet you feel relieved," Bob said on the way to the hospital.

Alice kept her eyes on the road and didn't say a word. They had driven long distances in silence before, but this was a different kind of silence, it was . . . charged.

"Alice, is something bothering you?"

Alice sighed, still staring at the road ahead. "I wish it didn't have to end."

Now Bob was totally confused. What was she talking about? It couldn't be chemotherapy. Although he had never experienced it personally, everyone had claimed it was a terrible ordeal. He cleared his throat, trying to buy time to come up with something sensible to say.

But before he could think of some nice words, they turned into the parking lot of the medical building and Alice's face lit up like a Hawaiian sunset. By the time Bob locked the car, she was pushing the call button of the elevator, and he practically had to jog to keep up with her. *Exactly what was going on here?* In the small, enclosed elevator cubicle, Bob noticed something else: Alice was wearing perfume, not just any perfume. "Are you wearing *Joy*?"

"Well, Bob, thank you for noticing." And with that, the elevator stopped, and Alice got out in a hurry. She made it inside the waiting room before Bob. As she was sitting down the receptionist noted, "You're our last appointment for today, Alice."

"Yes, isn't it wonderful?" Alice replied.

Bob just stood there. What did she mean by wonderful? was she saying that because it was *her* last appointment, or was there more to it?

"Go enjoy your coffee, Bob. We'll call you when I'm ready to be picked up," Alice said, while waving her hand in dismissal.

How about that! Bob went downstairs, sat at the outside patio with the book he was reading and soon became so engrossed in it that he forgot all about Alice's strange remarks.

At some point he realized he was the only one left on the patio and it was getting dark. Panicked, he checked his cell phone. It was on, but no one had called. He practically ran up the stairs, two at the time, and reached the chemo office just in time to see Alice standing by the door, hugging a tall man, in a friendly manner.

"Alice! How long have you been waiting?"

"I was just saying my good-byes to my wonderful therapist. Relax, you look flushed!"

In the meantime, the "wonderful therapist" had disappeared behind the frosted-glass doors and Alice slid her arm under Bob's as they walked toward the elevator. Bob didn't say a thing until they were seated in the car and leaving the parking lot.

"Does this wonderful therapist have a name?" he asked lightly, testing the waters.

"Eric, Eric Perez," she said in a dreamy voice.

"Hum, is there something else I should know about this Eric Perez?" Bob said.

"No, not yet, but I'm working on it." After that Alice began to feel sick, and soon Bob forgot about Mr. Perez as he helped Alice into bed, where she spent the next two days.

They were having their morning coffee outside on the terrace with the magnificent view. A light summer breeze flapped the newspaper, which Bob found extremely annoying but Alice remained unfazed. She appeared a little pensive. "Something wrong?" Bob asked.

"Nah, I have a lunch guest and was wondering if I should have something brought in. Then again, he insisted I shouldn't fuss. Decisions, decisions." She tapped her teaspoon against the glass tabletop.

"Do I know this guest?"

"Sort of. It's Eric Perez."

"The therapist?"

"See, you do know him. I finally convinced him to have lunch here instead of the coffee shop. I'm sure I can provide healthier food and it's so close to his office anyhow."

"I had no idea you two were still seeing each other," Bob said, then immediately regretted it.

"We aren't. Eric is married. He's also fifteen years younger." Alice didn't sound like she wanted to pursue the conversation. Bob got the message loud and clear.

Soon a pattern emerged. Eric Perez would have lunch at Alice's twice a week, Tuesdays and Fridays. Bob made sure he always had something going on these days, something that required his presence elsewhere. He also made sure he never asked direct questions, yet he still learned a lot. Alice was clearly smitten with this Eric, who was on his third marriage. He lived apart from his wife, and they shared custody of a fifteen-year-old daughter. Mr. Perez wasn't very good about keeping commitments or, as Alice insisted on calling it, lunch meetings. On the days when he didn't bother to show up, Alice was impossible to live with. But, on the other hand, lunch with Eric brought her days of happiness. Bob could understand her fascination with the man. He was handsome in a way. But he was also younger than Alice, not available, and had been her therapist. Yep, a match made in heaven.

It didn't hurt that Alice was filthy rich and very generous with her wealth. Eric began to spend some Saturdays over. Actually he would come over, get in Alice's Mercedes and the two of them would be gone for hours. Bob was aware they shopped, but Alice didn't come home with any merchandise. Maybe the purchases were all for Eric? After the man spent his first night with Alice, Bob decide he needed to have a frank talk to . . . clear the air. He also had a strong feeling that Alice was determined to avoid such "talk."

Another month went by and Eric Perez became a weekend fixture, to the point that Alice's grown kids started to ask questions. Linda, her firstborn and the one emotionally closest to Alice, called Bob asking what was going on. All the kids had noticed changes in their mother's behavior and while she seemed incredibly happy for now, they couldn't stop wondering "what if."

Linda invited herself to dinner on a weekday and insisted Bob be there, too. She didn't beat around the bush; her questions were direct and well-meaning.

"Mom, what's going on with this Eric Perez? I speak for all of us and you know we're only concerned with your well-being, so, what's up?"

"I'm in love. I've never felt this way before, no offense intended to your father. He was the love of my youth, and we had a family together, you kids. This is different; I can be selfish and take without really giving."

"Oh, for God's sake, Mom, who are you trying to convince? I bet you give plenty. But that's not what we're worried about. He's much younger and married. Where do you see this going? We're concerned you're going to get hurt."

For a while Alice just sat there, her hands folded in her lap, her gaze looking at a faraway point over the ocean. Then she spoke, her voice full of emotion. "I realize I'm older than Eric. Okay, much older. The fact that he is legally married doesn't matter. He is not living with the wife. He hardly sees her, and they're planning a divorce. I'm very aware you all think he likes me for my money. You aren't giving me any credit—not for intelligence and not for pride. It doesn't matter. When I'm with Eric, I feel twenty again. I feel invincible. I feel . . . complete. So while we may not last forever, what does? We might as well enjoy a relationship while it does last. I can accept that, can you?

"Let me tell you a story," Alice continued. "A young man passed by a car dealership every day on his way to work, and every day he would stop to admire a red two-seater in the window of the exclusive showroom. He would stare and dream. This went on for months. One late afternoon, as he stood sighing at the dream machine, the owner of the dealership stepped out and invited him in. Surprised and somewhat nervous, he followed him into the showroom. He stood in awe, inches away from the object of his desire.

106 ~ Maria Grazia Swan

" 'Like it?' the owner asked.

" 'Like it? It's more like burning passion!' the young man answered, blushing.

" 'It's yours to drive away,' the owner said. 'On one condition: You will keep it for only one year. You'll take very good care of it, never abuse it, provide a garage for it, and not lend it to anyone. And don't think I won't find out if you break the rules.'

"The young man stood speechless, thinking this was a joke. But the owner reassured him, 'Remember, only one year. When it's over, I expect you to bring the car back and hand back the keys with a smile. What will it be? Drive the car of your dreams for a year or never drive it at all?'

"He dangled shining keys in front of the young man's disbelieving eyes." Alice looked at us and then asked: "So what do you think? Should I take a chance for whatever length of time or should I give up love and happiness because it may not last forever?"

Soon Alice will celebrate her fifth year cancer-free; that's quite an important milestone. We have big plans for such a joyful occasion. All her family and friends will be there. Eric will be at her side for the celebration, just as he has been in these past five years. In the back of our minds—and I'm sure in Alice's—we know there's a risk that Eric may run off with someone else, or that out of the blue, he'll drain her bank account. Such is life. But for now, Alice is blissfully happy sharing her life with the man who helped heal her body and, more important, made her once again experience the magic of love.

Five Celebrity Baby Boomer Lovers

Naomi Judd

Birthday: January 11, 1946

Lover Qualities: Naomi used to be a nurse, no kidding. At a point in her life when people tend to retire, she formed a duet with her older daughter, Wynonna, and they went on to become country music's most famous mother-daughter team. The Judds scored twenty top-ten hits (including fifteen #1s) and went undefeated for eight consecutive years at all three major country music awards shows. In addition, the duo won five Grammy Awards and an array of other awards and honors. As a songwriter, Naomi also won a Grammy for Country Song of the Year with the Judds' smash hit "Love Can Build A Bridge." Her autobiography of the same name was a *New York Times* best seller.

In 1991, Naomi was diagnosed with hepatitis C, a potentially fatal chronic liver disease that forced her into retirement. She continues to keep busy being a humanitarian. The dictionary defines humanitarian as having concern for or helping to improve the welfare or happiness of people. How is that for love? According to her website, "service is the work of the soul and we're here to grow in love, wisdom and be of service." Naomi is active in programs like the Safe School Summit and the Women's World Peace Initiative. She's on the board of Mothers Against Drunk Driving, *USA Weekend*'s Make a Difference Day, a member of the Parents Television Council, and has donated her time and money to Kids on Stage (a local school program promoting the arts). In addition to helping start a hospice in her hometown, every Fourth of July the Ashland, Kentucky girl returns home for the Judd's Annual Food Drive to stock the Appalachia pantry. Both her daughters live very close to her home; it's a tight-knit family of women.

Trivia: In 1999 Naomi starred as Lily Waite alongside Andy Griffith in the made-for-TV movie *A Holiday Romance.*

Naomi also likes to clean. She claims that she scrubs her own toilets, and one of her favorite chores is doing laundry.

Naomi's real name is Diana. Both mother and oldest daughter changed their first names when they started their singing career. Diana became Naomi and Christina became Wynonna.

Love Life: Judd gave birth to her first child at the age of eighteen, then married and divorced in 1972. She became a nurse at thirty-one and a country singer at thirty-seven. Today she lives in Tennessee with her husband, Larry Strickland.

Suzanne Somers

Birthday: October 16, 1946

Lover Qualities: Somers is best known for her role as the ditzy blonde Chrissy Snow on the ABC sitcom *Three's Company.* But this lady has brains and heart. In 1971, while a struggling model, her young son was severely injured when he was hit by a car. At the same time, Suzanne was arrested for writing a bad check to pay her rent. But the negative publicity subsided once Suzanne explained the emotional and financial difficulties she was facing with her son in the hospital. On January 9, 2007, a wildfire in Southern California destroyed Somers's Malibu home, and all she had left was the clothes on her back. Appearing on television, Somers told reporters she loved her town and planned to rebuild. In March 2007, on *The Ellen DeGeneres Show,* Somers explained that she found her wedding band from her husband of twenty-nine years while sifting through the ashes of her home.

Trivia: Somers suffered from dyslexia as a child. After *Three's Company*, she's likely best known as the spokeswoman for Thighmaster, one of the first products responsible for launching the infomercial concept. She graced the cover of *Playboy* with a full nude pictorial twice: in 1980 and 1984. Somers announced in spring 2001 that she had breast cancer and she was treated with conventional surgery and radiation therapy. Instead of pursuing elective chemotherapy after her treatment, Somers chose an alternative therapy: mistletoe injections. Somers is also a supporter of bioidentical hormone replacement therapy.

Love Life: In 1968 Suzanne, while on the short-lived game show, *The Anniversary Game*, met her future husband, Alan Hamel, who was married at the time. The two began dating, and Suzanne became pregnant while Hamel was still married. They decided that Suzanne should have an abortion, which she did, suffering severe bleeding for several days. The two were married in 1977. Hamel was her business manager during the failed contract negotiations with ABC, which led to her departure from *Three's Company*. In spite of their rocky past, they are still happily together thirty years later.

Hillary Rodham Clinton

Birthday: October 26, 1947

Lover Qualities: In the summer of 1969, Rodham worked her way across Alaska washing dishes in Mount McKinley National Park and sliming salmon in a fish processing cannery in Valdez (which fired her and shut down overnight when she complained about unhealthy conditions). Rodham then entered Yale Law School where she served on the Board of Editors of the Yale

Review of Law and Social Action. During her second year, she worked at the Yale Child Study Center learning about new research on early childhood brain development. She also took on cases of child abuse at Yale-New Haven Hospital and volunteered at New Haven Legal Services to provide free advice for the poor. While First Lady of Arkansas from 1979 to 1981 and 1983 to 1992, she was active in a number of organizations concerned with the welfare of children. In 1997 she helped establish the State Children's Health Insurance Program and the Adoption and Safe Families Act.

Trivia: Hillary Clinton was listed as one of the one hundred most influential lawyers in America in 1988 and 1991. In her younger years, she earned awards as a Brownie and a Girl Scout. Clinton volunteered for Republican candidate Barry Goldwater in the U.S. presidential election of 1964. From 1978 until they entered the White House, she had a higher salary than her husband, Bill.

Love Life: Is Hillary Clinton a woman madly in love, the stand-by-your-man kind of woman or, as her detractors suggest, a shrewd politician, cynically staying in a failed marriage as a way of maximizing her own political power? I don't have an answer, only an opinion. I truly feel that Hillary would have achieved the same political success, with or without her husband; therefore, I believe she is a woman in love. Before they were married, she followed Bill Clinton to Arkansas, rather than staying in Washington where career prospects were best.

They bought a house in Fayetteville in the summer of 1975, and she finally agreed to marry him. Hillary Rodham and Bill Clinton were married on October 11, 1975, in a Methodist ceremony in their living room. She kept her maiden name until 1982. On February 27, 1980, Hillary gave birth to a daughter, Chelsea, her only child.

The state of her marriage to Bill Clinton was the subject of considerable public discussion. In November 1980, Bill Clinton was defeated in his bid for re-election. Publications printed claims that Bill Clinton had had an extramarital affair with Gennifer Flowers, an Arkansas lounge singer who came forward during Clinton's 1992 presidential election campaign, claiming that she had had a twelve-year affair with him. In response, the Clintons appeared together on *60 Minutes* during which Bill Clinton denied the affair but acknowledged he had caused "pain" in their marriage. (Years later, he would admit that the Flowers affair had happened, but to a lesser extent than Flowers claimed.)

In 1998, the Clintons' relationship became the subject of much speculation and gossip when it was revealed that the president had had an extramarital affair with White House intern Monica Lewinsky. When the allegations against her husband were first made public, Hillary Clinton stated that they were the result of a "vast right-wing conspiracy." She characterized the Lewinsky charges as the latest in a long, organized, collaborative series of charges by political enemies, rather than acknowledging any wrongdoing on her husband's part. To me, coming from a smart, educated woman like Hillary, this was love-induced naivety.

Faced with the incontrovertible evidence of his encounters with Lewinsky, President Clinton admitted to his unfaithful behavior. Hillary issued a public statement reaffirming her commitment to their marriage. Privately, however, she was reportedly furious with him and was unsure if she wanted to stay in the marriage. A woman in love or a shrewd politician? I'd like to think a little of both.

Terry McMillan

Birthday: October 18, 1951

Lover Qualities: This successful writer gave all of us single boomers high hopes of finding new love in unexpected places. *Waiting to Exhale*, which remained on the *New York Times* best-seller list for many months made McMillan a star, but it was

How Stella Got Her Groove Back that made her a lover. Based on McMillan's real-life romance with a much younger man, the book and subsequent movie starring Angela Bassett had every woman over forty booking a trip to Jamaica.

Trivia: McMillan worked at a library when she was sixteen.
Her favorite colors are orange and purple.
McMillan raised her son as a single mom.

Love Life: Unfortunately McMillan's happily-ever-after is still in the making. Terry married her young stud, who several years later announced that he is gay. A very ugly divorce followed. But hope lives on, and I understand Jamaica is still a popular vacation destination among single boomer babes.

Katie Couric

Birthday: January 7, 1957

Lover Qualities: Couric seems to constantly try to make us take better care of ourselves. Doesn't that sound like motherly love? After the death of her husband, Jay Monahan in 1998, Couric became a prominent spokeswoman for colon cancer awareness. She underwent a colonoscopy on-air during *The Today Show* and inspired many others to get checked as well. In other words, she used her grief to help others.

Trivia: Katie Couric was the voice of news reporter "Katie Current" in the U.S. version of the film *Shark Tale*. She guest starred as herself on NBC's *Will & Grace* in late 2002. Couric was the first female anchor of any of the "big three" weekday nightly news to broadcast solo. Couric has won multiple television reporting awards throughout her career, including the prestigious Peabody Award for her series *Confronting Colon Cancer*.

Couric is one of only seven women to have been repeatedly ranked among the world's most influential people by *Time* magazine.

Love Life: Couric dated jazz musician Chris Botti but they reportedly broke up in February 2005. She was previously and has intermittently been linked with multimillionaire TV producer Tom Werner.

Whitney Houston

Birthday: August 9, 1963

Lover Qualities: Whitney's singing career is spectacular. And the majority of her greatest hits are songs about love. "I Will Always Love You" is still the biggest hit single in rock history. Even her first tour was titled "The Greatest Love." With all that singing about love, it should come to no surprise than when Whitney did fall in love, everyone knew about it. Remember the roller coaster years of her marriage to Bobby Brown? If there ever was the perfect lover-with-blindfolds, it's Whitney.

Trivia: Houston's first cousin Dionne Warwick and Houston's godmother, Aretha Franklin, are notable figures in gospel music, rhythm and blues, and soul music recordings. Houston began to perform at eleven as a soloist in the junior gospel choir at her Baptist church. She sang background vocals on Chaka Khan's hit single "Papillon."

In the early 1980s, she appeared as a fashion model in various magazine advertisements and made the cover of *Seventeen* magazine. Houston's performance of "The Star Spangled Banner" at Super Bowl XXV in 1991 was released as a single and reached the top twenty on the U.S. Hot 100. Houston donated her share of the proceeds to the American Red Cross.

Love Life: Bobby Brown and Whitney were married from 1992 to 2007, which in show business is an eternity. And a very colorful union it was. How can we forget that photo of Whitney wrapped around Bobby the day he was released from jail? But all that drama took a toll on her career and her life. We all wish Whitney many more years of love.

The Diehards

The Diehards

Susan called today. A welcome surprise as Susan isn't the type to call just to kill time or gossip about our sisterhood. The last time our Boomer Babes got together, we were a little harsh on her because of her tendency to get involved with "unavailable" men. That's our code name for men who are married or committed—to a relationship, not an institution. From our soapboxes we preached to our wicked sister, and Susan didn't even defend herself.

These days, she is setting up her own life-coaching practice, and she called looking for ideas on new marketing strategies for her business.

"You know, I'm thinking about using a motto, a slogan, something people could remember me by. The competition is fierce; anything that will set me apart would be wonderful." Susan's voice sounded a little sad.

"That's a great idea, Susan. How about: *'Give me an hour, I'll give you a life'*?"

Her laugh sounded great; I hoped I cheered her up. "Promises, promises," she said. "I can't promise what I can't deliver, but it is very catchy. A lot better than what I had in mind."

"Which is what?"

"Insanity is doing the same thing over and over expecting different results."

Uh, oh. That was, in a nutshell, the subject of the discussion-turned-ugly at our last lunch.

"Funny you should say that. I'm sitting at my computer reading what I wrote yesterday. I'm using the same quote, but the more I think about it, the more I think it's bunk."

"Did you say bunk?" Susan asked. "I never expected that word from you, my friend."

I ignored her. "Doesn't 'If at first you don't succeed, try, try again' sound familiar? Isn't that encouraging people to keep doing the same thing? Yet, nobody bad-mouths that old saying. Why?"

"Interesting," Susan said.

"Interesting? I think it's brilliant. No, I mean, I'm brilliant. Think about all the nice people who never give up but are getting a bad rap from the rest of us. It's the same story as the glass half-full or half-empty. This isn't only about relationships; it can impact all aspects of our lives. It's not like somebody wakes up one morning and decides, okay, today I'm inventing the lightbulb, or the Jacuzzi, or Viagra—that's so close to our . . . hearts. Each new discovery is the success that follows many failures."

"True, but there's a big difference between products and people."

"Susan, think back to your first bicycle. It may have come with four wheels to give you that safety edge. At some point the two extra wheels had to come off, and I'm sure your parents kept warning you to be careful. Like the rest of us, you paid no attention and fell off the bike once or twice. How am I doing so far? I don't know your parents and I can't tell you what role they had initially on your bike training. Maybe after you skinned your second knee, they chose to take away the bicycle until you were older or maybe they encouraged you to keep trying. You see where I'm going with this. Regardless of whether we were the daredevil toddler or the scaredy-cat one, we all grew up and now have to make our own choices. Chances are very good that the trailblazers among us were once the toddlers ready to try anything. Or, if all fails and the attempts persist, we might label her or him a diehard. That's not fair because deep down inside, we all share the same goal: we want to succeed."

"Hmm, I think I see where you are going with this. So in reality, I'm getting involved with married men because my parents took away my bike when I was a toddler."

Silence.

"Go ahead, Susan, make fun of me but you know what I mean."

I heard a sigh at the other end of the line. I waited.

"I'm going to use *Give me an hour, I'll give you a life.* That's a trailblazer's decision. Correct?"

Now I'm the one laughing. "Susan, I'm no shrink, but I have the feeling we may see you riding a two-wheeler any day now."

"Mistakes are part of the dues one pays for a full life."
—Sophia Loren

If at First You Don't Succeed . . .

A Quiz

Please read the following statements and mark one of the following: Agree (A), Somewhat agree (S/A), Disagree (D). Keep track of your choices as you progress.

1. People who volunteer are either very rich or very old.

    Agree (A)   Somewhat agree (S/A)   Disagree (D)

2. If you want something done fast, give it to a busy person.

    Agree (A)   Somewhat agree (S/A)   Disagree (D)

3. True love will find you when you are not looking.

    Agree (A)   Somewhat agree (S/A)   Disagree (D)

4. You have to kiss a lot of frogs to find your prince.

    Agree (A)   Somewhat agree (S/A)   Disagree (D)

5. The only way to get out of the hole is to stop digging.

    Agree (A)   Somewhat agree (S/A)   Disagree (D)

6. It takes two to tango.

    Agree (A)   Somewhat agree (S/A)   Disagree (D)

7. You can't judge a book by its cover.

    Agree (A)   Somewhat agree (S/A)   Disagree (D)

8. The road less traveled is generally unkempt.

    Agree (A)   Somewhat agree (S/A)   Disagree (D)

Time to add up your score.

If you have six or more S/A answers, you are one lucky person. You have enough openness of mind to look at both sides of the coin before deciding on the value. And you are patient in a world where people's attention spans are sometimes shorter than Mariah Carey's miniskirts. Patience is a virtue—congratulations.

If you have five or more A answers, you are a laid-back kind of person. In general, you tend to be agreeable—more because you don't want to argue than because you are convinced that the other party really has the best solution. Sooner or later, you'll stumble on something worth arguing about and that could change your outlook forever.

If you have five or more D answers, you are a little on the controlling side. That may serve you well in work-related matters, but it may also prevent you from forming long-lasting relationships. Keep a mental picture of that half-full glass; it may help soften your perspective.

If you are one of the people with mixed answers, and you feel you don't fit any of the above groups, don't panic. You may or may not be a diehard, and that's why the last quiz in the book will help you decide to which group you belong.

No matter what your answers, remember: most of the things in life that we accept without questions are the result of our own attitudes; the ones we developed in our early years. If we adjust our attitudes, the outlook may change for the better. Here are my words of wisdom: if the printing seems a little blurry, before you go buy new glasses, wipe clean the lenses of the ones you're wearing. You may be pleasantly surprised.

If Looks Don't Matter . . .

You need new glasses.

Ever wonder what would happen if two diehards of the opposite sex became attracted to each other and decided to live happily ever after? Together, I mean. Well, we are about to find out. Here is Mary Anne's story.

We are sitting at our regular table, the usual suspects minus two. Lisa called from her car to say she was stuck in traffic on the west side of town and wouldn't be able to make our lunch, after all. Mary Anne is also late, but that's to be expected: she is a nurse for a skin specialist and sometimes patients' appointments ran overtime. Mary Anne is our youngest member. Sam, who puts tags on everything and everyone, named her "Cusp Babe." In astrological parlance, the "cusp" is the time between the end of one astrological sign and the beginning of the next. Since Mary Anne was born at the tail end of December 1964, I guess the nickname is appropriate. She has been attending our lunches off and on for about six months now, but has revealed very little about herself. Which makes us a little crazy with curiosity. We are all amazed and a little envious of the fact that she can eat anything she wants and doesn't seem to gain any weight. Kathy thinks it's because she's never married or given birth.

"It's true," Kathy is explaining, "for some reason people who have never been married seem to be thinner. Maybe they socialize more, you know. They go hiking and dancing whenever they want with whoever they want."

The rest of us shake our heads in disagreement. Kathy has

lately begun to wax nostalgic about being single, even though *she is* single. She's decided that a single divorcée's life is somehow tainted compared to marriage virgins, right down to the tendency to be a little plump.

Finally, here comes Mary Anne, without a trace of makeup, pink cheeks, bright smile, a mass of healthy, glossy chestnut hair and, I swear, a true "hearty" look about her. She says she never uses any products that contain dye or perfume and we believe her. Just look at her! How else could she look so pleasingly wholesome?

Mary Anne is the kind of person who can blend in with any kind of crowd. I don't mean to be catty, but she is sort of generic, in a good way. However, the exception to the rule is that she doesn't really fit in here, among us. She sits to my right, with her beige, long-sleeved top, a perfect match to her cotton pants and her open-toed flats. Her only jewelry is a gold chain worn around her neck, with a tiny gold cross. To my left sits Susan, who makes enough racket with her bangles and dangles to rattle a mummy out of its sarcophagus. And every single one of us is wearing a trendy, colorful outfit, even Sam who often wears simple, tailored clothing.

"I may be moving." Mary Anne's announcement comes out of nowhere.

"You're moving? Do you need to sell your house?" Michelle, the Realtor, doesn't miss a beat.

"No, I'm renting, month to month. And, I'm not buying a house, I'm moving in with my—" Mary Anne hesitates looking at us from behind her thick glasses, and we are all holding our breath, she is moving in with . . . ? "I'm moving in with my fiancé," she concludes.

We look at each other with astonishment. None of us even knew she was dating. What a mystery woman!

"Congratulations!"

"Good for you."

"Tell us more!"

"Who's the lucky guy?" We are all talking excitedly, and people from other tables are looking at us.

Then she says: "Robert Kline." And our table goes completely silent. Once again no one is breathing.

Sam is the first to find her voice: "*The* Robert Kline?" Robert Kline is the local version of Donald Trump—same attitude, different do. A picture of this man and Mary Anne together flashes in my mind's eye and my brain clicks "delete."

"Isn't he married to that weather girl from channel twenty-one?" Sam asks.

"Divorced," Mary Anne replies.

The rest of us are still staring in mute dismay. "What was that, wife number ten?" Sam asks. I kick Sam lightly under the table, and she frowns at me.

"Number four," Mary Anne says, in the same unfazed tone. "Before that there was the Hollywood starlet, then his child's sitter, followed by the Argentine model, and finally the TV weather girl."

"You're going to marry him?" This time my foot makes more forceful contact with Sam's shin. She looks at me in disbelief. "What? You got restless legs syndrome?"

I shake my head while Mary Anne says, "I don't believe in marriage." The Cusp Babe is full of surprises.

"Why? Is it against your religion?" Sam is still the only one talking—though I am communicating, albeit ineffectively, with my foot.

"Not really. I like my independence. Plus, there's something about signing your name on that dotted line. Everything changes. I'm convinced that the blending of happiness and marriage is an unsustainable condition." *Whoa, that's a mouthful!*

"I thought you said you've never been married."

"Correct. But I don't need to be. All I have to do is look around. There are over twenty-four million single boomers in the United States and more than nine million of those have never married. Don't you think there is a good reason for it? I've known people who live happily together for years, they get married and six months later it's over. They end up in an ugly divorce." Okay, well, we now know why she never married.

"Is that what happened to your fiancé's marriage?" Michelle gets up the courage to ask. What a strange question, I thought. *Your fiancé's marriage.* How bizarre.

"No, he found the weather girl in bed with his secretary."

"Robert Kline's secretary is a man?" *Please, Sam, shut up!*

"No, his secretary is a woman." Aye, ye, ye. Time to change the subject. "Actually, it was a gift from above," Mary Anne says. "Robert finally saw the light. He's done chasing young, immoral eye candy. He is ready to settle down and commit."

"And not a day too soon. What is he—ninety?" This, coming from Kathy with her perfect comic delivery, provides some much needed relief. We all breathe a sigh of relief and laugh, even Mary Anne.

Now that the interrogation is over, we discuss older men and younger women in a civilized fashion, although we leave with the distinct impression that Mary Anne doesn't have a clue what she is in for. We kiss her cheeks, wish her well, and ask her to stay in touch.

I miss the next lunch but make it to the next, though I'm very late and end up just having dessert. On my way in, I cross paths with a platinum blonde dressed in an emerald green silk pantsuit.

"Well, hello!" this woman says to me. I stop, look more closely.

"Mary Anne?" I say. "Wow. You look so different. What inspired you to change your look?"

She gives me a nervous smile. "Yeah, I was telling the rest inside, Robert was annoyed with the length of my hair. It was getting in the way of our—lovemaking." Her cheeks are on fire, and she keeps her eyelids lowered behind her thick glasses but goes on talking, "I visited a hair studio he recommended, and they ended up drastically changing my style." *No kidding. And who changed the rest of you?* "Well, got to run, it was nice seeing you," she says, and disappears through the revolving doors, a swirl of luminous silk under a platinum blond bob.

I join the rest of my boomer friends on the dining patio, and I'm still disturbed by the encounter with Mary Anne. I order a glass of wine. Mary Anne is, of course, the topic of the day. I'm not listening to concerned plain talking—it's more like a mass snickering about her looks and what Mr. No-more-eye-candy-Robert managed to do to her. I'm guessing we aren't going to see the old Mary Anne back any day soon.

"This is really freaking me out. Why would someone get involved with a person and then proceed to change her into someone else?" I ask, not anticipating a direct answer.

"He was a patient where she worked as a nurse," Lisa says. "Need I say more? Deep down inside Robert Kline is probably just a big baby. He was going through a messy, public divorce and had a bad rash, possibly stress related. Here comes Mary Anne to the rescue. I bet she's a very caring soul, a big difference from his past women. I don't know, have we all forgotten about how opposites attract?"

"Well, if opposites attract, apparently that attraction has worn off," I say, but no one is paying much attention; a gorgeous silver-haired man just entered the dining room, and we are all staring at him.

Two months later I ran into Mary Anne at Fashion Square Mall. I left my car at the Nordstrom parking garage with the intention of looking at some shoes when someone called my name. I sometimes have problems recognizing people because I refuse to wear my glasses unless absolutely necessary. The voice sounded familiar, so I walked toward the woman, a smile on my lips, and I figured that by the time I reached her, I'd remember her name. I didn't. The woman had a short, spiky white-blond hairdo, bright red lipstick, heavy blue eye shadow, dramatic eyeliner, and what appeared to be fake lashes. Keep in mind I wasn't wearing glasses, so if *I* noticed the lashes, they had to be the glue-on kind.

"How are you? So nice to run into you." She hugged me! *Who is she?* "It's me, Mary Anne."

"Mary Anne? 'Cusp Babe' Mary Anne?" Her laugh told me I'd hit the bull's-eye. "Wait, wait, let me get my glasses." She had on so much perfume I sneezed. I fumbled through my handbag, found my glasses and a piece of gum. "Let me look at you! My oh my, I would never have recognized you." She was still blond, but a lot of other things were new. "Your eyes; I mean, your glasses?"

"RK," she said, nodding and chuckling.

My eyes traveled down her outfit, back to her chest. "Hey did you—?" I cupped my hands over my chest in the universal sign language for large breasts. She nodded and laughed even louder. She'd had breast implants? Okay, enough with the joke; will the real Mary Anne please come out of hiding?

"Are you ladies still doing lunch? I've been meaning to come by but I'm so busy, so much has happened. I'll call you. I have to run. I have an appointment with the ophthalmologist. I'll call, I promise." And she was gone.

I was left there, glasses hanging low on my nose, the gum stuck to the roof of my mouth, and my mind in total chaos. I had to tell somebody. I had to share this before I started believing it was just a figment of my imagination. Fake eyelashes? Fake boobs? I never made it inside Nordstrom's. I sat in my car dialing the Boomer Babes; this called for an emergency meeting.

We decided to get together for drinks. Lisa's house was the most centrally located, so we met there.

"Lisa, I can't believe it." I was still in shock. My wine was untouched. Somehow I felt as if Mary Anne had died or something. "She didn't look like herself at all. She looked like an older version of that weather girl. Remember? Robert Kline's last switch-hitting wife?"

"I'm not surprised. What's that old saying? A leopard may shed his fur but not his spots? Why would Robert Kline go from young, flashy girls to Mary Anne? More important, why would a nice, intelligent person like her be attracted to someone like him? Do you think it'll last much longer?" Lisa asked.

"Hell no! Don't you people read the papers? He is all over town with some showgirl from Vegas." I had no idea Sam was so up-to-date with the social scene. Go figure!

Then it hit me: poor Mary Anne must be dying inside. She let the jerk change her and now she is all alone. I pulled out my cell phone and without saying a word to the audience, I dialed Mary Anne's number. Lo and behold, she answered at the second ring.

"Mary Anne, it's me. Are you okay?" Well, that didn't come out the way I wanted.

She must have recognized my number on her caller ID because she spoke in a lovely sweet voice. "Of course I'm okay, I didn't mean to run out on you like that, but I really had an appointment." She lowered her voice. "A very important appointment. I'm getting married." She hadn't lost her knack for off-the-cuff announcements.

"Married? You're getting married?" Now all the Boomer Babes crowded around me, trying to listen in. I had to fight to keep Kathy from grabbing the phone away from me. "You mean you and Mr. Kline are getting married?"

Even Lisa, who was in the kitchen, could hear Mary Anne's laugh. "That old goat? No way. I broke up with him months ago."

"But your new look, your breasts, the lashes . . ." Her loud laughter took on an edge of hysteria. My ear was hurting.

"Okay, here is what happened. I have to talk fast because I'm driving to the restaurant. Once I get there I'll hang up. I'm meeting Eric, my future husband. Robert was bound and determined to change me into one of his eye-candy girls and I went along because I *liked* it. Until he decided to fool around with my eyes. He wanted me to get contact lenses. I had tried that before, and it didn't work with my eye problems. But he wasn't giving up. He bought me a plane ticket to Los Angeles and made an appointment with a well-known eye specialist. I was so angry and knew I wasn't going to put up with his bullying anymore, but I went. Then I met the doctor . . . it was love at first sight. Eric did surgery on my eyes and now I get by with contacts. I broke up with Robert and thanked him for introducing me to the love of my life. Eric is in town, and I'm meeting his mother. I'll send you an invitation to the wedding. I'm here, got to go." She hung up and I put my hands over my ears to fend off the shouting and questions from my curious sisters.

Next week I'll start shopping for a new outfit for Mary Anne's wedding.

Looking for a perfect ten only guarantees strained eyesight.

She Trusts Me, She Trusts Me Not

It's all about loose marbles.

Most people will agree that trust is an important part of love. In Beverly's case, I don't know which canceled out the other. Did she stop loving because she couldn't trust or did she stop trusting because she didn't feel loved? Here is her story. You be the judge.

I'm sitting in Beverly's kitchen, sipping tea and chatting. The TV is on with the sound turned way down so we can concentrate on watching her mom doing her thing. Ana, Beverly's mother, sells skin products on one of those home-shopping channels. She's been doing that for over ten years, a real pro. I met Ana on a few occasions, always at Beverly's.

"Do you really think there's cactus juice in her products?" I ask.

Beverly smiles. "Mother says there is. Who am I to doubt my own mother? She's been selling her wares for a long time, and it has to do some people some good or they wouldn't be buying it the second time around. As long as it sells I get to live here rent free."

"Here" is a sprawling one-story older home on the outskirts of Scottsdale. Ana bought it years ago and uses it as her business base. Cacti juices, home in the desert—it's a good image for her products.

"Your mom looks good." I sigh. "How old is she? She looks at least ten years younger than me, than you too for that matter."

"True," Beverly agrees. "She's always had a fabulous complexion. Maybe it's because of her Asian lineage?"

"That and the fact that she's so petite." I look at Beverly, a good five-seven.

"Mom is coming to town next month, and I need to put together a very elegant party. She's bringing some investors because they are talking about going international. It's such a bore, but it's the price you pay for free rent."

"Can I help? Please, please! It's not like I have buyers and sellers lined up to look at properties. And I love your mom's parties," I say.

Beverly gives me a strange, serious look, the way you assess an item before buying it. "I guess I could use some help. I'll have to cancel some classes." Beverly teaches her daily yoga classes on the front porch, which she converted into a studio by enclosing it with large French doors and installing air-conditioning.

The rest of the house is off-limits to the students; they are allowed to use the powder room, period.

I've known Beverly for a long time; we became close after I passed the "bathroom test."

This is now an inside joke between us, but unfortunately, with trust being such a big issue in Beverly's life, it really isn't a laughing matter. I'm not sure what caused this, but at some gut level, I feel it has to do with her father. The only time I innocently asked, "So, where is your dad?" she stopped whatever she was doing, gave me this long, somber look, and said, "I don't know, and I don't care to know." Her voice was so cold and cutting I wasn't about to mention her father again any day soon.

I come here when I need a refreshing course for my soul, because it is remote, in an urban sort of way. You can hear the birds, see the butterflies, and watch the occasional coyote stroll the grounds. The whole place smells of incense and clean living. I started out as one of her students, but now we're close friends. I'm hoping there's more to it than the "bathroom test."

Beverly, who is mistrusting and suspicious of everything and everybody, keeps glass marbles inside her guest bathroom's medicine cabinet. This is not a novel idea; I've heard and read about it many times, although the thought of actually doing it never crossed my mind. Beverly claims that over 75 percent of the people using other people's bathrooms will, at some point, open the medicine cabinet. I never did. She also keeps a huge toy snake, like a giant coil, in her linen drawer in the same bathroom. Once you let it out, good luck on making it small again. It's not that she has a warped sense of humor; she has a phobia of some kind.

I remember once she had out-of-state guests, and her mother asked her to make them feel at home until she got here. Since the house belongs to Ana, Beverly couldn't refuse. Before the arrival, she asked me to go shopping with her; we went to some international market store, where she bought a dozen little golden bells on silk ropes. When we went back to her house, I helped her tie a bell to each inside door handle. That way, even at night she would know where her guests where coming or going. Bizarre, but also clever. That day, while securing the bells to the doors, we spoke about men, namely our former spouses. Beverly had two, one more than I did. But while I had been married a long time and had kids, both her marriages were brief and childless.

"My first husband was a dentist," she said. "We met in college—my first year and his last. In retrospect, he was a very nice man. I broke his heart."

"Why did you two get divorced?"

"I got pregnant right away. It was a miserable pregnancy; I was sick a lot, and he was just starting his practice. I lost the baby before the end of the term. It was a little boy. I filed for divorce the day I got out of the hospital."

"You did? Why? Was it something your husband did?"

"No. Now I can look back and say, no. He was hurting as much as I was, but in my mind, I blamed him for everything; that made the whole ordeal easier to accept." She paused and seemed to stare at some imaginary point in the distance. For a moment I could "feel" her pain; then it was gone, and Beverly was back to hanging bells.

"So, what happened after that?"

"I didn't want to move back with my mother, so I left my husband's house with just the clothes on my back, got in my car and drove until I ran out of gas. For a few years, my life was a living hell. I moved around, stayed with friends, got into ugly relationships. Then I moved in with an older gentleman who treated me like a princess. He was the one who encouraged me to learn yoga. He paid for my classes, sort of gave me an education. He also gave me an STD. Turns out I wasn't the only princess in his life.

"My mother was trying to talk some sense into my head, but I wasn't ready to listen yet. Every man I hooked up with turned into a disappointment. There was Joe—I found him in bed with the teenager next door. With Luis, I found a used condom while cleaning the bathroom, and we didn't use them. The last straw was Adam. He invited me over to his place for the weekend. I was so excited that I bought a lovely pink nightie for the occasion. We had drinks, foreplay, went into his bedroom. Then he turned down the bedcovers, and there were obvious blood smudges on the sheets. We looked at each other, and he muttered, 'Sorry, I scratched my leg. I'll get clean linens.' I didn't know what to do. I went into the bathroom and right there in plain sight in the wastebasket was a soiled tampon. I grabbed my clothes and was out the door and in my car in my pink nightie." Beverly looked at me. "Now you know why I don't date. Make sure those bells are well-secured."

"Yes, ma'am!" I didn't ask about the last husband. I had an urge for fresh air. Poor girl. I still couldn't figure out the connection between cheating men and the bells, marbles, etc. Was it plain phobia or deep fear?

It turns out it was a little of both. One of the men she broke up with wanted revenge and came back to attack her in the middle of the night. He got into the house in spite of the alarm system, but it alerted the police, who arrived before her ex-lover could get to Beverly, who had locked herself in the bathroom. For months after that, she would cover the floors with pots and pans before going to sleep, a trick she'd learned from a friend in the police force.

Beverly's house guests are arriving tomorrow, and everything is ready. Her mother is bringing two men. Most of the party guests will be staying in the nearby hotel, but the two major investors will be at the house. Ana wants to make sure she is in total control. I'm on the phone with Beverly. "Are you sure you don't want me to come early and help out?"

"No, you've done enough. Make yourself pretty and come to the party. Mom says one of the European investors is single and about our age, so spruce up your Italian. I'm not sure what language he speaks, but I noticed how you Europeans always stick together."

"Yeah, yeah." I don't have the nerve to ask if she got rid of her glass marbles and her golden bells, but I know her mother will have a fit if something goes wrong.

I see the lights and hear the music and the chatter even before giving my car to the valet. Whoa! Ana must be pleased. Beverly did a great job. And there is my friend in a lovely pale blue chiffon dress, looking relaxed and smiling at me as I come up the pathway. I grab a glass of bubbly from a tray as Beverly walks me from guest to guest.

"Wait until you see Oliver," she says.

"Oliver?"

"Remember the investor from Europe? The one who's single?"

Just then I see Ana. Her ebony hair is pulled back into an elegant coif. She is talking to a tall man in a dark suit. Beverly gets all giggly on me and presses my elbow to make me walk faster.

"Oh, so nice to see you," Ana greets me. "Let me introduce you to Oliver Dalton."

So, this is Oliver. "A pleasure to meet you," he says. He sounds like Sean Connery. My legs are weak—whoa, Beverly is right.

I mingle, I chat, and I notice something different about Beverly, an inner glow. Is she happy to see her mother or is it something else? Dinner is served in the enclosed porch, and the caterers did a wonderful job. I'm sitting at the same table as Ana and Mr. Dalton. Beverly's seat is at the next table, but she is hardly sitting; she moves around and checks on the servers.

Mr. Dalton is telling me that he flew in from London, a direct flight with British Airlines. His jet lag is beginning to show. "I have a bit of a headache," he says.

"You should take an aspirin," Ana says. "It helps me when I'm traveling."

From the corner of my eye I notice Beverly motioning me over, so I excuse myself. "How is Oliver?" Beverly whispers in my ear. She is acting like a teenager, and it hits me: she likes the Englishman.

"He's fine. He has a headache—jet lag. I need to get back before your mother misses me." I'm on my way back just as Oliver gets up and walks away.

Ana says, "He's going to the bathroom to get some aspirin. That's where Beverly keeps it, if I remember correctly."

And then it hits me: dear God, what if Beverly forgot to remove the marbles?

Crash! The noise is so loud that I assume he must have left the bathroom door open while going for the aspirin. The whole room is silent. I recognize the sound of cascading marbles from the tile counter to the tile floors.

Beverly, face pale, rushes toward the bathroom, her heels clip-clapping on the tile floors and then, *bam!* We all hear the scream and another crash. A different-sounding crash of a body landing on the tiled floor. Ana and I are off our chairs and on our way to the bathroom. Beverly is on the floor, her lovely dress in complete disarray. She has a pained look on her face and fire spitting from her eyes. She is swatting her arms like a windmill, fighting off Oliver who is trying to help her up. "You, you!" Beverly's finger points and pokes poor Oliver's chest.

I bend down and whisper in her ear, "Your mother sent him in to get some aspirin."

"Huh?" Now she is looking at me with a lost look in her

eyes. She looks at me, at her mother, at Oliver, and suddenly she starts to sob. Great! Ana must be thrilled.

By the time the paramedics arrive, Ana has explained to Beverly why Oliver was in the medicine cabinet. Beverly apologized for the ugly names she called him, and we all had a double helping of bubbly. Beverly badly bruised her tailbone—and her pride. She will need to lie on her stomach for a few days, but all in all she is okay. Call me a chicken, but I figure this is a good time for me to keep busy and stay away for a few days.

When I come by one afternoon to say hi, I nearly drop dead when Oliver, in jeans and a polo shirt, lets me in. I don't ask what he is doing there; he is obviously busy removing the golden bells from the doorknobs. Beverly, on a chaise lounge, sips tea and smiles with the idiotic expression of a person in love.

"What's going on?" I ask.

"We're removing the bells," Oliver says. "I don't know which feng shui book Bev read, but it's wrong. The bells do not bring good luck when placed on the doorknobs."

"It could've fooled me," I say, winking at Beverly. "I had no idea you were in town," I add, looking at Oliver.

"Yes, still checking out some info connected with the business." He speaks with the Connery voice and I can listen to him all day, but I won't. His cell chimes, and it's Ana, so Oliver steps away to talk shop.

"Do you need anything, Beverly?" I look at the tiny bells, glistening inside the cardboard box where Oliver put them. "Want me to take the box and donate the bells to the thrift store?"

Beverly doesn't answer; she is avoiding my eyes. Then she takes a long breath and in a strange tone of voice says, "No, better I put them in storage; one never knows when they may come in handy."

I nod, kiss her cheek, and walk toward my car. Then I turn around and wave to Oliver who is standing on the porch. "Bye, Oliver, good luck to you." He waves back and gives me a happy—oh, so happy—smile. He doesn't have a clue what the good wishes are for. I hope he never has to find out.

"When he is late for dinner and I know he must be either having an affair or lying dead on the street, I always hope he's dead."
—Judith Viorst

Is Sex a Four-Letter Word?

Who wants to know?

Some people are addicted to alcohol, others to drugs. Then there is the workaholic, the shopaholic, and the Internet addict. Connie's addiction was sex. And she was hooked before her twenty-first birthday. Here is her story.

Fresh out of high school, Connie went to college on a scholarship. Her parents, Italian immigrants, were so proud of her that they gave her a car for her twenty-first birthday. Her two-year-old Ford Mustang convertible instantly became the talk of the neighborhood.

On this particular weekend, Connie parked her Mustang on the street side of her parents' house. Everybody else in her family had gone to a cousin's place for a baptism, and Connie was home alone. Her friend Tony stopped by to say hello. "Hello" apparently meant having sex in Connie's parents' bedroom. It was not the first time for either one of them. Unfortunately, her parents came back in the middle of the tryst. Tony, who was on a brief break from the seminary, panicked, and jumped out the second-story window, landing on—and crashing through—the Mustang's ragtop. He twisted his ankle in the process.

Life at home would never be the same after that. Connie packed her things and moved to the East Coast. Time went by. Connie got married, had a couple of kids, got divorced, and went to work as an editor for a big publishing company. Her kids grew up, moved out, and then Connie opened her own literary agency. Through all of this, one thing remained constant: Connie's craving for sex.

In her younger years, she may have reacted to infatuation,

chemistry, or plain lust. Now, as she grew older, she didn't need any of that for enticement. She found herself having sex at the most inopportune times, in the most awkward places, and with the most inappropriate people—and for all the wrong reasons. Her husband found her in bed with his boss; her kids walked in while she was busy performing oral sex on the high school coach; and although she was never fired for it, everyone knew she had regular sex with her young male assistants. Note that the word "regular" is used to define frequency and not position.

Once Connie became a literary agent, she moved back to California. She was approaching fifty and wanted to be closer to her roots. With her looks fading, she found herself alone a lot. Although she wasn't aging gracefully, her appetite for sex was just as uncontrolled and unleashed as ever. Connie now had two sources for sexual partners: the Internet and her profession. As an agent, she would prey on the aspiring authors seeking representation. Through the Internet, she had access to all types.

I met Connie through her profession. She never did represent me as an agent, but we became friends and we socialized. I realized how out of control her addiction was when she told me she practiced unprotected sex. No kidding.

"I'm not going to die of AIDS, I know it. Sure I get scratchy, itchy stuff from time to time. So what? I will not get AIDS." This from an intelligent, educated woman. Pure nonsense.

"Connie, are you crazy? You have no idea who the people you sleep with have slept with before you." While it may have sounded hokey, I was trying to get through to her. "Do you have a death wish or something?"

"Yeah, to die of indigestion with the largest penis possible in my mouth." Well, she didn't use "penis." She used a more colorful word, but I'd be embarrassed to repeat it, and I'm not a prude.

Connie had a lot of sex, but no love at all. While in a general sense she could be viewed as a predator, she had her share of bad encounters. I remember when she met Dick—no snickering, it was his real name. They met through a chat room on the Internet. Connie told me he was a movie producer who had a house on the beach. The next thing you know, her phone calls are transferred to his line and she is practically living there. Once a week I would collect the carloads of mail she received from all the hopeful writers and delivered them to the gate of the luxurious enclave. She would meet me there.

"Hey, Connie, when do I get to meet the man? By the way, the people at the post office are very annoyed with you. They say you need to check your box more often."

Connie would laugh, transfer the mound of manila envelopes to her car, give me a hug, and disappear down the manicured private road leading to her secluded paradise.

When I finally got my wish to meet Dick, it was in a courtroom where he was being tried for fraud, stolen identity, theft—you get the picture. Connie was one of his many victims. By the time it was over, she had to declare bankruptcy. Since she had to relocate, she decided to move closer to her parents' old home. Her daughter was now living there and running the family olive business. They did talk to each other on the phone, but not very often. In an unusual act of goodwill, Connie offered to babysit her only granddaughter, Desiree. Big mistake.

"Why, Mom? Are you hoping to meet the coach?" her daughter asked. Short answer, long memory.

With her babysitting career shut down before it even started, a mellow Connie called me that day. I hadn't heard from her in a long time. She wanted to spend the weekend with me, just to talk, she said.

I could tell by her voice, she had hit bottom. We met in Hermosa Beach, halfway between her place and mine. We spent the day walking on the sandy paths, and I did the listening.

"I don't like sex." Connie's statement left me speechless, for—let's say—a nanosecond?

"Gee, Connie, you could have fooled me, that's for sure. What's this all about?"

"I'm an old woman. I've screwed up my life and the lives of

others because I've refused to handle problems. Sex is my cure-all. Other people take a tranquilizer; I have sex. Okay, it's truth time. I never wanted to admit that I was ruining other people's lives with my actions. My justification was this: if I'm having sex with another adult—a consenting adult—who am I hurting? When I look back, I realize I have hurt a few people."

"A few people? Connie, if you look back, you'll see the path of destruction you left, wide and long enough to take you to China or hell, pick your destination."

"I want to make amends. I want to change. Help me." The desperation in her eyes was real.

"There isn't much I can do. You need to do it yourself. I think they have support groups, like they have for alcoholics—you know, the twelve-step programs? I bet you can google it. You have sex with the same ease and frequency as other people brush their teeth. You really need help from experts, not from me."

We walked side by side silently for a long time; then Connie started to talk about the latest literary trends and the subject of sex and redemption seemed to fade away.

She called me a month or so later. "Hey, girlfriend, my granddaughter is having her First Communion and guess what? I'm invited." Was that Connie on the phone, before sunup? I bet she never went to bed.

"Congratulations. Connie, it's 6 A.M. Couldn't this have waited? What are you doing up so early?"

"Early? The sun is shining over the ocean, birds are singing, life is good."

"Shut up. Have you been drinking? No, you're not slurring. Are you on speed?"

"Nope, getting ready to go to my volunteer job."

"Huh?" Connie working for free? Doing what? Taking sperm from young donors?

"That's right; we haven't spoken in a while. I joined the support group you recommended." I was getting credit for recommendations? What recommendations? "That was six months ago, and I've been celibate ever since. Okay, I may have slipped once—wait, if you do it twice the same night with the same man, does it count as one slip or two?"

"Connie!"

"Sorry, sorry. So, my daughter wasn't going to let me see my granddaughter. She even turned down my offer of free babysitting. Imagine that. Like I let people tell me how to live my life. I didn't complain, didn't say a thing. I went to Desiree's school and signed up as a crosswalk substitute, a volunteer. That means that if the regular paid person has a problem, I cover for her. Well, Gertie, the sweet old lady doing that, suddenly developed a bad, recurrent hip problem. At first I begrudged my daughter for forcing me to get up early, but then I got the routine down pat. I stop by Java Paradise, grab a large coffee, bring a folding chair and a book and watch these cute, noisy little tikes walk to school. Desiree is the cutest one of all. At first I just waved at her. After a while I said hi. Then I decided it was taking too long for recognition so I began to bring along Tusk, my dog."

"You have a dog?"

"I would tie the leash around the light pole, give him plenty of water and munchies, and watch the kids going into slow meltdown every time they walked by. Soon, some of them would bring Tusk treats."

"You have a dog named Tusk?"

"Yes, why so surprised? It's a mutt from the animal shelter. He has a strange tooth poking out, and Tusk sounded appropriate. Anyway, the little ones just love to pet his head and he licks their little faces and lets them look at the tooth. It's so precious. So one day—"

"I'm sorry, I'm still stuck at the part where you say you have a dog named Tusk. You hate pets, all kind of pets—too much trouble, you always said."

"People change. I've changed; get over it. As I was saying, one day Desiree comes by and she has a brown bag in her hands. She pulls out a huge treat and gives it to Tusk. Then she smacks a kiss on his head, right between his ears. As she leaves, she says, 'Bye doggie. Bye Gramma.' Thank God I had that folding chair. My knees buckled. I had to sit down. I think I was hyperventilating. She called me Gramma. She knew me. I kept my cool but now when she crosses, I give her a special smile and say, 'Have a good school day, Desiree.' I didn't know what to do next. It turns out I didn't have to do a thing. My daughter called me and said she heard about my school crossing job. She said Desiree was fond of Tusk, and my daughter suggested we meet and talk."

"Connie, what can I say, this is so gratifying."

"The First Communion is next Sunday, and I have to get a new outfit. Want to go shopping with me?"

"Love to. Wait, does this mean you're not a literary agent anymore?"

"Are you nuts? Of course I am. What do you think I'm going to pay for the new dress with, doggy treats? Got to run and help those lovely children cross the street. Catch you later. I have so much more to tell you."

She hangs up, but not before I hear a loud barking in the background. Must be Tusk. Wonder what breed he is. More important, is she going to keep the mutt once she is back in good terms with her daughter? And how about the newfound celibacy? It's one thing to kick a bad habit; it's much harder to stay the course. I want to go back to sleep, but I remember what Connie said: "The sun is shining over the ocean, birds are singing, life is good." I get out of bed, put on my sweats, and go for a jog. One day at a time. Works every time.

"You mustn't force sex to do the work of love or love to do the work of sex."—**Mary McCarthy**

To Russia for Love

Can't buy love? Lease it.

Dan is a rare diehard—a happy diehard. Even though he ends up alone over and over again, he continues to dive into relationships again and again, even hopeful.

Here is Dan's story, as told by my friend and fellow Boomer Babe Susan.

I met Dan on the Internet a few years ago when dating sites were still somewhat a novelty for the privileged few and computers weren't as abused as they are today.

On a hot July evening, out of boredom, I decided to take advantage of a free-week offer from a popular matchmaking site. The site had a separate section for "silver foxes," singles over fifty. I sat at the computer and browsed through hundreds of photos and profiles of men who claimed to qualify as silver foxes. What fun! All I had to do was fill out a profile form, and voilà, I became part of the silver foxes romance pool.

One hour and one glass of Chardonnay later—after declining the offer to post my photo free of charge and shaving a few years off my birth date and a few pounds off my weight—I was done. Time to go to bed. By morning I'd forgotten the whole thing.

As we know, computers don't forget. The following day, I found a message announcing I had mail. What an adrenaline rush! Indeed, three gentlemen had sent me "a cyber wink." The ball now in my court, I checked out the profile of each winker, but replied only to one who caught my attention.

That's how Dan and I began our cyber correspondence. We exchanged e-mails, then photos and phone numbers. We spoke on the phone about once a week for a very long time; we never ran out of things to talk about. We had both been married once, for over twenty years, then divorced. Both Catholic, although not practicing. Our adult children no longer lived with us. We even shared the same zip code.

I confess, I was smitten even before meeting Dan in person. It seemed like I was living my life to the beat of Dan's calls.

These weekly conversations went on for a while, and I had to fight the urge to ask him out. (All this before *He's Just Not that into You* hit the nation's bookstores to become an overnight best seller.) But I was wise enough to figure out on my own that I should let Dan set the pace. The way I read him, either he was killing time waiting for something better, juggling several prospects or, and I was rooting for the later, just cautious.

By the time September rolled around, Dan asked me if I'd like to meet for an afternoon cup of coffee. Would I like? Thrilled. The minute I hung up the phone I found myself dancing around like a silly teenager. I spent days going through my closet, deciding what to wear. I hadn't felt so alive in a very long time. By sheer luck, I had lost a few pounds and now I was the same weight I had posted on the matchmaking site.

We'd arranged to meet at a bakery/coffee shop in the food court of the local mall. I spotted a man resembling Dan's description standing in line at the bakery counter. Even from the back I instantly knew it was him. I took my time to study the man who had managed to make my heart sing before we actually met. Tall and thin with a full head of silver hair; he wore jeans and a black polo shirt.

I walked over and stood behind him in line. When he reached the counter and ordered his coffee, I said, "Can you make that two? Two cups of coffee, please."

Dan turned around, the surprised look on his face quickly becoming a pleased grin. I hoped he liked what he saw.

We sat and chatted for hours, like old friends reunited. Seems we both had sons in the marines, both of us subscribed to the local paper, liked to sleep in, shopped at the same grocery store, and lived only blocks away from each other. Before saying good-bye, he promised to call. I went home and called all my girlfriends to announce I'd just met Mr. Wonderful.

Days went by and no call. Should I call him? I decided to play the waiting game; I liked him way too much to let my lack of patience blow any future possibilities. He was worth the wait. When he finally called me weeks later, he explained he had been out of town to visit family. He invited me to breakfast. A first!

"Pick where you'd like to go," Dan said on the phone.

"IHOP?"

"IHOP? You kidding? Susan, it is my very favorite breakfast place. Pick you up at ten."

And so began a new tradition. Twice a month Dan would invite me to breakfast, and I would reciprocate by inviting him to a home-cooked meal at my house. He would bring a bottle of wine, and we'd have a pleasant time. I quickly realized that while I was financially comfortable, judging by Dan's address and the assortment of luxury cars he drove, he was quite wealthy.

My girlfriends and I spent hours trying to decide if the breakfasts at IHOP qualified as dates. But since no physical contact, not even hand-holding took place, the unanimous consent was no. When he came for the monthly dinner Dan would walk around my house and never fail to notice even the smallest changes, a new pillow, a larger plant. However, with the exception of the dinners, we never met in the evening. This was driving my girlfriends and me crazy.

"Maybe he has a secret lover stashed in the dungeons," kidded my suspicious friend Brenda. "Stop by his house late at night unannounced and see."

I wasn't going to do that.

"What if he's gay?" said Lisa.

I doubted that. Why post your profile under *Men seeking women* if that's not your interest?

"I think he's cheap," said Juel, who herself was married to a miser who squirreled away every penny for a rainy day. If you're a native, you know it never rains in Arizona. "Pay attention to what he tips at breakfast," she said. "That will be the telltale."

It was a clever suggestion and at our next IHOP "date," I paid close attention to Dan's actions. He didn't leave a cent for the server. Score one for Juel: the man was cheap.

Thanksgiving came and went without change, and Christmas lurked around the corner. I decided to be bold and ask Dan if he would like to go to Midnight Mass with me. "I'm going to a party on Christmas Eve," he said. "But I may be able to do both. Sure, count me in. We can work out the details later."

While elated that he would go to church with me, I was a little disappointed that he mentioned a party without inviting me. He often met my friends when he came to dinner, but I realized I'd never been introduced to any of his friends, I wasn't even sure he had any.

We attended Mass at the Casa de Paz y Bien, a Franciscan retreat center. It was an emotional and uplifting experience. Nothing could spoil my perfect Christmas Eve, I thought.

Dan appeared in a great mood during the drive home. "You'll never guess what I did this week," he said. "Got myself a passport."

"Congratulations. What's the occasion?" Dan knew I had a trip to Europe coming up and I waited in anticipation of the answer I imagined, *To go to Europe with you, my dear.*

Instead, he said: "I'm going to Russia, possibly next month."

Something in his voice put a cramp in my bowels. *Russia?*

Out loud, I asked, "In the middle of winter? Is it a matter of great urgency, or are you a masochist?" I doubt my sarcasm even registered; he appeared giddy with excitement.

Suddenly, I knew. It had to be one of those Russian Internet sites, you know, *beautiful young women want to meet you?*

I didn't say anything, but when we arrived at my house, I mumbled something about a headache, wished him a Merry Christmas, and ran inside. I didn't want to believe he could be so foolish, but the realistic me knew better.

After a good cry, I realized that my first instinct had been correct. Dan's search would never end. The grass would always be greener on the other side, and right now the other side was Russia. To him, I was just a comfortable person to have around. I doubt he realized he hurt my feelings. Hurt my feelings? More like broke my heart. Later, when he called, I asked if he knew somebody in Russia. He vaguely mentioned . . . a friend.

"Are you going to stay with your friend?"

"No, no, I'm renting a room in someone's flat."

"You're renting a room? From someone you don't know? Is it like a bed and breakfast?"

"No, it's just a room. I'll eat out a lot, with my friend." Dear Dan, cheap to the bone. I couldn't help wondering if IHOPs did business in Moscow.

We carefully avoided the subject of Russia after that, but our relationship changed. I knew we were never going to be anything more than friends. I had to decide if that was okay or not.

Off to Russia he went for about a month. After his return, he called and invited me to breakfast; he wanted to show me photos of Russia.

When we met, I received a warm embrace. Russia or not, Dan cared about me in his own way. He had tons of photos. A blond woman appeared in some of the photos. She was very thin, wearing dark business suits. She looked to be in her early thirties, attractive but not particularly beautiful. She could be a legal secretary in any American office. Not at all the siren I had imagined. He always referred to her as "my friend"—no names.

"So, how was Russia? Did you have a good time?"

"Not really. I doubt I'll do it again, but if I did, I would plan my vacation differently, maybe visit the countryside."

I refrained from asking too many questions, but here is what I gathered: He spent twenty-one days in Russia on the outskirts of Moscow. He didn't rent a car. He rented a room in two different flats because the people needed the money, but were too crowded to let him stay longer than two weeks. He only ate out with "the friend" on four occasions. The rest of the time his meals consisted of snacks purchased in Russian grocery stores.

Now you can see how cheap Dan could be.

I didn't need to ask if the friend was planning on seeing him again. Dan was a cheapskate even by poverty standards. Months went by before he would openly talk about the lousy time he spent in Russia and my assumption proved to be correct—he traveled all the way there to meet the Russian woman he'd connected with on the Internet.

Now, you would assume Dan had learned a good lesson. But you would be wrong. By now, no more Mr. Wonderful. Instead, just plain Dan. And soon to become Poor Dan in my eyes. Part of me wanted to smack him silly, the other part knew there wasn't much I could do to make him see the light, especially since Dan was still very much into young Russians. But now he found a way to meet them without flying to Russia.

The next one came from a local matchmaking site. In her forties, she'd been married two years to an American who imported her from Russia. Two years later, the marriage was over. He tossed her out on the street. She posted her profile on the Internet, and two weeks after the first contact she moved into Dan's home and into his bed. I found that out when he showed up for dinner with a "guest" named Natasha.

Let me pause here and ask if I'm the only one who wonders why almost every Russian girl you meet in the States is named Natasha? Once I met two sisters and each one introduced herself as Natasha. How strange is that?

This Natasha (or whatever her name is) was skinny, about five feet tall, wearing inexpensive, tight-fitting jeans, a casual top, and too much makeup. Mostly I remember that she had angry eyes. She hardly spoke, hardly ate, and kept rubbing against Dan. I was relieved when they left, and knew I would never invite Dan back to dinner. I can't say I was jealous, but I felt strangely protective of this man I had come to think of as a friend. In all honesty, he was a good friend and willing to help me in many ways. He never hesitated to give me a ride or offer good advice on matters he was knowledgeable about, but romance would never be a viable option between us.

A few months later Dan, alone, stopped by my house to show me his new Corvette. He owns about four luxury cars and I don't know how many Harleys, but this Corvette was indeed a showstopper. I noticed something different about his face: he looked younger and healthier. It wasn't because he changed his lifestyle; it was cosmetic intervention. Good for him, I thought. On impulse, I ran up to his car as he was leaving and asked if all was good. He hesitated, then said, "Maybe it's time for a little breakfast at IHOP. Tomorrow's okay?"

"Tomorrow sounds perfect." His shiny black Corvette roared down the road. The next morning we sipped coffee waiting for our pancakes to be served. Dan told me he had to ask Natasha to leave.

"Why?"

"It's her family," he said.

"Oh." Okay that wasn't a cleaver answer, but I was very surprised. I'd had no idea she had family in the States.

"First, her daughter," Dan said. "Her sixteen-year-old daughter was living in Russia with the grandmother. I lent Natasha money for the plane ticket to bring her here. She said she'd pay me back a little every month. You know, she works at a department store now. Well, the girl showed up with the grandmother, and they settled in my house. They constantly speak Russian, and I felt left out. Natasha quit her job and started driving them around town with my car and my gas."

Ouch, his car and his gas. I had to hold my paper napkin over my mouth to hide my Cheshire smile. Hey, that was not revenge, it was . . . fair play.

He went on. "One night, they dragged me to dinner at this Russian restaurant where we ran into a woman working there as a waitress. Turns out she is in the country illegally and needs a place to stay. So now *she* is in my house. They've taken it over. It's not just the underwear and pantyhose drying in my shower, or the disgusting tampons in my kitchen garbage can. It's the constant chatter in this foreign language. They are all so loud. I think they talk about me, and not in a nice way. I can't stand it. I could have stayed married if that's the way I wanted to live."

By the following week, the women had left Dan's house and moved into a three-bedroom condo owned by an older gentleman. I'm not sure which one of them kept the master bed warm for its owner.

As for Dan, he is now a member of the Russian social club. From time to time, some young Russian woman moves into his house. They never stay long, but he seems content. He tells me they are usually good cooks and keep his house clean. Natasha visited him recently. She now lives with her daughter and her American boyfriend. The grandmother went back to Russia. Natasha had an accident and totaled her car. She spent a few days *and nights* at Dan's house, and then he loaned her one of his older cars. Over breakfast last week Dan told me how upset his kids are that he squanders his money on young Russian girls. Here is how he put it: "I'm aware they're after my money. So what? It's my money and I can spend it any way I like. They get money; I get great sex. Beats hiring an escort service, and I get home cooking and a clean house to boot. So, who is the fool? I'm renewing my membership at the Russian club."

I miss the old days when time and Mother Nature had a way of leveling the field between mature men and women. Today, with Viagra and similar pills, unless the men run out of money or Russia runs out of Natashas, they can keep the game alive for many years to come.

"The most important thing in a relationship between a man and a woman is that one of them be good at taking orders."—Linda Festa

The Paradise Valley Monthly Book Club

Don't judge a book by the cover.

Paradise Valley is to Phoenix what Beverly Hills is to Los Angeles. Most expensive dirt in the county, and the houses resting on it are usually the size of resorts, with resort price tags attached.

Adjectives used to describe the homes in the township of Paradise Valley vary from elegant, secluded, one of a kind, opulent, classic, impressive, and magnificent, to the other end of the spectrum: flashy, obnoxious, showy, gaudy, pretentious, and tasteless. Words you'll never hear associated with them include: quaint, cozy, small, simple, or affordable. It is probably the Arizona town with the most gates, outside of Florence, where the majority of the state's prisons are found.

Yet, Paradise Valley is no different from any other town in the United States. Okay, well, maybe a little different. I do believe it is the only town without a grocery store or gas station. But that said, the people living in these large houses are people like you and me. There are a lot of nice people in Paradise Valley and some not so nice, just like any other place. The Paradise Valley Monthly Book Club is a great sampler of nice women. About twenty of them. They started the club years ago, when their children were in school and the moms wanted something safe and rewarding to do outside the house, one evening a month. Now most of the children are grown, married, or in college, but the women still meet to discuss books. Some of the faces have changed over time, but more or less they all fit the same demographic: over fifty, comfortably well-off, and sheltered by similar gratifying routines.

Christina is the youngest member of the club. In her early fifties, she has that strange beauty that defies the classics. If one were to analyze her features, her eyes would be too far apart, her nose too thin, her forehead too flat. Yet, put it all together and Christina has the timeless look that still beguiles a lot of young men. And that is the focus of her constant complaints: the age of her suitors.

A few years ago, out of the blue, the Paradise Valley Monthly Book Club decided to read Rachel Greenwald's *Find a Husband After 35*.

While they all were over thirty-five and some were indeed single, none of them was actually yearning for a husband. But it was summer in Arizona, the temperature outside was 112 and Linda, the hostess of the month who had suggested the title, made superb margaritas, so they all agreed, Greenwald's book it would be.

The monthly meeting fell at the end of September on an unusually breezy evening that had a full moon to boot. So lovely was the evening that the women decided to take the discussion outside by the pool. The moon's rays shimmered on the water, and the tequila lightened their moods even further. Everyone felt relaxed and chatty. Ten minutes into the discussion, their conversation began to transcend the primary subject. It started with Trish. She objected to everything about the book, including the title. Trish was embroiled in a messy divorce and proclaimed that men over thirty-five only look at women under thirty. Apparently her husband had been carrying on with a young secretary.

"You can't bunch all men together because of one bad apple," said Jennifer, who was a newlywed at the time.

However, the "disgruntled woman" floodgates had been flung wide open. Each and every one of them had a story to tell, and it didn't matter how long they had been married, divorced, or even widowed. The margaritas flowed, and the tales of discontent gushed.

"I had to get larger implants to keep my Mr. Piggy happy,"

said Lorie, pointing to her tremendous breasts. "Him and his kinky sex, it's killing my back."

"I can relate. My husband gives new meaning to 'bringing your work home,'" said Louise, rolling up the sleeves of her white, crinkled cotton blouse to expose red marks around her wrists that looked like bruises from handcuffs. Whoa! Her husband was the town sheriff.

That shut everyone up for a minute, until Christina said in her low, breathy voice, "The only men who ask me out are all much younger than I am."

The rest of the book club exchanged glances, perhaps considering dipping Christina into the deep end of the pool, head first, to punish her for complaining about something that sounded like a bonus.

Lorie piped up. "You should be thrilled that younger men find you attractive, as long as you keep your checkbook in a safe place you'll be fine. Have a good time, and enjoy it while you can."

"You just don't get it, do you?" Christina's eyes darted from face to face. "You all think they're after my money. Do you think I'm stupid?"

A chorus of "No, no, of course not" filled the air. Feeling a little guilty and a lot intrigued, the women asked Christina for more details. As it turned out, she seemed to have always been irresistible to younger members of the opposite sex. It started in high school when she was a senior and only juniors asked her to the prom, and it culminated with her current ex-husband. He was five years younger and had left her for an older woman. How humiliating can that be?

"I was still being carded at thirty-five," she said, "and now that I'm over fifty, if I ask for a senior discount, I have to show ID. That's so unfair." Most of the women in the room would have killed to have her problem, but they were all intelligent and caring enough to keep their mouths shut.

From that evening on, the monthly book club meeting became more of a get-together for gossip and real-life stories than for fiction discussion. They all felt that reality was far more interesting. Christina's life alone was exciting enough to keep them all entertained.

First she dated Robert, Bobby to his friends. She met him at the Catholic Alumni Club winter gala. Since Christina is not Catholic, she had no idea this was a singles event. She drove a friend who'd had her driver's license revoked for DUI, thinking it was another company Christmas party. Bobby spent the evening following Christina around and being extremely attentive. She gave him her phone number before leaving with her intoxicated girlfriend. He called and soon they began to see each other regularly. Bobby was romantic, worked as a social worker for the city, made very little money, did not constantly pressure her for sex, and was thirty-four years old.

Every month Christina reported their progress, or lack of it, to the book club members. They were all suitably touched when she told them that Bobby took lunches to work for months to save money to buy her an iPod, which he had loaded with her favorite songs. Never mind that she could purchase three iPods with what she spent on her haircut, manicures, and pedicures each month.

They were all surprised when by the fourth month she was ready to call it quits. She told the ladies of the club she felt like a teacher dating her high school student. And he never got physical. There was a lot of cuddling and foreplay, but no sex. This had seemed sweet at first, but had grown weird with the passing of the weeks. Now, all of this happened before the movie *The 40-Year-Old Virgin*, so when Christina brought up the subject of Bobby's lack of libido, and her suspicions about him being gay, no one objected. When she broke Bobby's heart, all her friends in the club cried for him.

However, as time went by and new young men entered and exited Christina's life, a pattern emerged. Four months seemed to be the magic number for her relationships. No matter how perfect and idyllic the affair appeared to the club members, Christina always found faults serious enough to result in a breakup about the fourth month into the relationship. And yes, Christina always did the breaking up.

She also had a real problem with letting anyone meet her boyfriends. Louise, who had stopped wearing long sleeves to the meetings, since everybody knew about her bruised wrists anyhow, suggested Christina talk to one of her friends who was a counselor. Christina refused; she went to a tarot-card reader instead, and was told that the love of her life was just around the corner.

At a late spring meeting of the club, the women discussed staying in shape as you aged. Most of the women were on some kind of exercise program, from basic walking to advanced pilates. Christina had just joined a new yoga studio and couldn't stop talking about it. "Look," she said, standing up, "I think I've grown an inch in height since I've been going there." Everybody laughed, but there was no stopping Christina. "I'm telling you, the stretches are so intense, if done correctly and with the right frequency, they restore your height by realigning your spine. I didn't believe it either when Adam told me, but it's true. Adam was right." There was something about the way she said the name Adam that got everyone's attention. Her tone changed, and her eyes went dreamy.

"Who's Adam?" The question came as a chorus, followed by, "How old is he? Is he married?"

"He passes the age test," Christina joked. Passing the age test meant he was at least seven years older than her son. "He is not married," she continued, "but I'm not dating him . . . yet."

This mysterious yoga instructor was fueling the women's imaginations. The stereotype presents images of tall, lean, lithe bodies moving gracefully from pose to pose. If any of them contemplated the idea of signing up for the yoga class, they were wise enough to resist temptation. Among the book club members, the yoga studio became known as "The Garden of Eden" and the forecasted romance as "Christina's Earthly Delight."

By the time the June get-together approached, the ladies of

the club could hardly contain their curiosity. But the day before the meeting, Christina called the designated hostess to announce she couldn't make it because she was flying to Las Vegas with Adam to attend a yoga convention.

That evening, the club was abuzz with the news. Not for a minute did they believe the yoga convention excuse. After all, isn't Las Vegas famous for quick weddings? Most of the meeting time was spent planning a reception for the newlyweds. Would Christina be registered somewhere? These women were very content with themselves. They all felt like matchmakers, despite the fact they'd never met the alleged groom. And they weren't going to wait a month to find out about Las Vegas. Lorie, who, although not that much older, had elected herself Christina's fairy godmother, called her on the phone.

When asked about Vegas and wedding chapels, Christina erupted in cheerful laughter. No, of course there was no wedding, but yes, she had had a wonderful time with Adam, and they were now officially dating. The news spread fast, and the ladies called a secret meeting, unknown to Christina, and plotted how to meet Adam. They would have a fabulous Fourth of July party and insist Christina come with her date.

Christina wasn't so easy to convince. She kept saying maybe. She'd probably never have gone to the party had it not been for something that happened a few days before. She was out by the pool alone. Her son was in Texas visiting his dad when Adam stopped by her house in the late afternoon to drop off something she had left in his car. They ended up having fabulous sex. By the time they showered, it was dinnertime, and Adam suggested eating at one of the trendy Scottsdale restaurants. She could pick whichever one she wanted. Christina said she'd rather have some pizza delivered. Pizza delivery is not one of Christina's habits, and Adam knew that.

He was quiet for a minute and then asked, "Are you embarrassed to be seen with me in public?"

"Of course not, silly," she said. But something in her voice gave her away, and he wasn't about to let it go.

158 ~ Maria Grazia Swan

"Am I not good enough for your friends? Is it the way I dress?"

"No. Why do you say things like that?"

"Because I just realized that while in Vegas we went everywhere together, but when we're in town, you have a tendency to keep me undercover. Do you intend to hide me in your bedroom forever?"

That was just too much for Christina. Still under the magic spell of the sexual marathon, she relented. "Look, there is a party at a friend's house for the Fourth of July. Why don't we go together?"

And so it happened, on the afternoon of the fourth, sporting clothes handpicked by Christina, freshly shaved and wearing Christina's favorite aftershave, Adam walked into the lives of the ladies of the Paradise Valley Monthly Book Club and shattered all their preconceived ideas of what a yoga instructor looks like. Adam was short—only two inches taller than Christina—on the stocky side, with a full head of curly hair and an everlasting devilish smile on his face. Forget the tall, silent, spiritual chanting type. He was funny and entertaining. A big hit. When they sat down to feast on barbeque, an out-of-town guest complimented Christina on her "charming husband." She quickly set the woman straight while Adam, hiding a grin, patted her hand under the table.

Time went by, and at the end of the fourth month, when the relationship had taken on an air of old news, Christina called Lorie and told her she was going to break up with Adam because he had lied to her. Since Christina sounded pretty distraught, they decided to get together and talk about it. Adam had lied about his age; he was two years younger than he had told her. "For this you're going to end a great relationship?" asked Lorie.

"There's more," Christina said. "He's been married and divorced. When he was twenty-one he married a family friend who was in her forties and they were divorced five years later."

"So? I was divorced before I met my husband. Does that

make me a bad person?" Lorie was puzzled, even more so when Christina confessed that he had actually told her about the divorce months before and had explained that he fibbed about his age because she had told him about the "test," and he didn't want her to reject him before she actually had a chance to get to know him. Christina and Lorie spoke for hours. Lorie reminded Christina that times have changed; older women and younger men are acceptable—look at Demi Moore and Ashton Kutcher, Susan Sarandon and Tim Robbins. When she finally left, Christina promised to think about it. Then she went straight to the yoga studio and told Adam they were done.

For the following weeks, every day was a sad story. Adam sent flowers; she threw them away. She refused to talk to him and wouldn't take his phone calls. She wouldn't open the door when he came by. Then one early morning, she went to get her paper and there was Adam, sitting on the doorstep; he had been there all night. They made up. Christina told Lorie, who told the rest of the group. But somehow they all knew this wasn't going to last. It was almost as if Christina was searching for a reason not to be happy.

Sure enough, the final blow happened on Valentine's Day. Adam surprised her by picking her up in a limousine and taking her to dinner at his yoga studio. He had hired a chef, a string quartet, the whole shebang. After the incredible candlelight dinner, he got down on his knees, brought out a diamond ring, and asked Christina to marry him. To which she simply said, "No," and got up and left. Thirty minutes later Adam showed up at her house ready to break down the front door if she didn't let him in. To avoid a public display, Christina unlocked the front door.

Here is how she described the following scene to the members of the book club the following month:

"Why won't you marry me? I thought you loved me."

"I do, it's just that—"

"People who love each other want to spend the rest of their lives together, Christina."

"I understand, but I'm not sure I'm ready."

"You mean you are not ready to get married now? Christina, we don't need to rush, I can wait. I love you, I'm simply looking for some sign of commitment."

"I could adopt you," said Christina, and she was only half joking.

They looked at each other for a long time. Adam's eyes became very sad. He bent his head, slowly turned around, and left Christina's house and her life forever. Not long after that, taking advantage of the hot real-estate market, Christina sold her home and moved to Texas. Lorie talks to her by phone from time to time. For awhile Christina went into therapy. Recently she was dating a rodeo cowboy who barely passed the age test, but we all know how old those young bronco riders are. The ladies of the club are marking their calendars. The fourth month is coming up.

"Never mistake motion for action."—Ernest Hemingway

The Crying Game

It's your party, you can cry if you want to.

Kim attracts men by playing the damsel in distress. She has a real knack for "milking" the strangest situations. We are not friends, though over the years, our paths have crossed. I've noticed her manipulative ways on more than one occasion. Recently, her fabricated predicaments became reality. Some people would call it karma. I like to think of it as what goes around, comes around. Better yet, getting a taste of your own medicine.

We met for the first time many, many years ago at a support group. Both in our late thirties, both newly divorced. I was legitimately struggling with my divorce, but Kim, in retrospect, may have been lying even back then. On that Sunday afternoon, we sat in a circle—eight women, three men. My divorce still so new, I felt extremely vulnerable and transparent. We sat on folding chairs with our ankles properly crossed and our hands resting nervously on our laps. We took turns sharing our broken dreams and our lost tomorrows. The list of causes and effects that brought us to that circle to share our grief was only so long—but some of us are better storytellers than others—and in our group, it was Kim. What was a divorce case became, in her own words, a journey of courage—hers—and of cold persecution, from her ex. With lots of peculiar details in between.

The group met in a religious setting with a friar as the moderator. To some of us, this was one more cause of discomfort. We passed around a large plastic heart with a crown of thorns. I know, I know, it sounds kooky, well it was—but hey, when you are in pain, you'll grab on to whatever you can in hopes of easing that pain. When the plastic prop landed on your lap, it was your turn to share your story. The prop made its way around the room and although Kim wasn't the last one to share the thorny heart, she may as well have been.

Had I not known better, I would have said that even the chairs had been designed for special effect, to set off Kim's petite body. I'm guessing she was a size 0, and she had short blond hair and expensive designer threads in soft pastel colors to complement her light, flawless complexion. Enough bling to let you know she's got it but not too much to look gaudy. I was too far away from her to tell you what she smelled like, but I'm sure it was a light, alluring scent. And as I said, she was the only one in the room to look at ease on the plastic chairs.

Kim stroked the heart with her slender French-manicured fingers, let out a soft, long sigh and looked up; exposing our naive psyches to her incredibly beautiful blue eyes.

"Hello, my name is Kim." Her voice sounded childlike and just like in that movie, she had them at "hello." By them, I mean the men in the room. All three of them. By the time she got to the part where her husband's mistress stole all of poor Kim's clothes, Angelina Jolie could have come marching through the room followed by an entire orphanage of teenage girls in cheerleader uniforms and none of the testosterone kings would have blinked an eye.

While the men bombarded her with comments like: "How were you able to get away from Colorado with your child, without a car, clothing, or wallet? You poor, poor, darling, courageous lady."

Yep, we were women, but Kim was a lady. We, the women, listened to this story of martyrdom and also had questions: "Kim, just what are the odds that your husband's mistress wore your size, or for that matter, liked your clothes? Was she into recycling? And why would your ex come with a U-Haul truck to take your furniture and your car, but let you keep the kid and the credit cards?"

Kim turned her lovely face in our direction, batted her long lashes, let out another sigh, and totally ignoring our sarcasm, said, "Al, my husband, only likes petite women." Of course, she said this as her stare moved up and down the large, plump frame of the unfortunate woman who dared to question her. The men never caught on to that dig; they were too busy trying to figure out how to ease poor Kim's sorrow.

There was a positive side to all of this. For a few hours, all of us women forgot our troubles and united in our distrust of Kim. A few of us remain friends to this day. After the session, we walked to our cars and watched Kim getting very chummy with Rocky, one of the three stooges from the group. I knew Rocky from before—our kids had played in the same Little League and although not close friends, we were long-time acquaintances. His wife died after a long illness, and he had just started to get out again. He was a nice, decent man. My first impulse was to call him on the phone and warn him about "ladies" like Kim, but by the time I got home, fed the dogs, and watched the news, I forgot all about Kim and Rocky.

Months went by, and I ran into Kim at a chamber-of-commerce mixer. She looked . . . luminous. Men flocked to her. I walked over to say hi. She looked at me like I was an alien from outer space. "It's me, remember? From the group, at the Casa?"

She kept on staring without uttering a word. I could feel everyone's eyes on me; they must have thought I was some lunatic, or one of her ex's mistresses. I turned around and left.

The image of Kim staring me down bothered me a lot more than I cared to admit. Maybe I'm a forgettable person, or maybe she didn't want to be reminded of something associated with me? After I got home, I called one of the women I had met at the same support group and told her about my encounter.

"Better not let Rocky know you saw her," Elaine said.

"Rocky? Why?"

"Apparently they dated for quite some time, and then she left without telling him, but she did take some souvenirs."

"What kind of souvenirs?" I had a sinking feeling in the pit of my stomach.

"Some of his dead wife's jewelry, his car, and his heart. He's pretty devastated over the whole thing."

"Oh, my, I had no idea. Do you think she is a scam artist?"

"I doubt it. I think it is more a sense of entitlement. You know, like, she's better than the rest of us and should be rewarded for sharing herself with others?"

"Do we know her last name?" I asked Elaine.

"I'm sure Rocky would know. I mean, he was planning on marrying her. Why do you want to know her last name?"

"I have a friend who is a private detective. He owes me a favor."

"You wouldn't!"

"I would and I will. Get me her last name."

Of course, I expected real life to work like the detective shows on television. Make a phone call, click a few buttons and pronto, someone's private life shows up on the computer screen in Technicolor. Wrong.

My friend the PI called me a week later. "Your girl is squeaky clean," he said. "She moves around a lot, had five different addresses in the last two years, owes a lot of money to a lot of people, but all her credit cards are current. She was married once, almost twenty years ago, but it only lasted six months and that was back in Alaska." *Alaska? What about the mean, cheating ex in Colorado?* "Well," my friend continued, "she may break a lot of hearts but she doesn't break any laws."

We all forgot about Kim and went on with our lives. I got my real-estate license, my kids moved out, and I moved on.

One weekday during spring, I was on my way to Paradise Valley to show some properties when I noticed a car on the side of the road. It looked like a Jaguar—pale green. Must be a woman's car, I thought. I slowed down to see if the driver needed help and pulled out my cell phone, just in case. The driver's side window was rolled down and as I slowly drove by, a woman's face appeared. She motioned me to keep on going, flashed me a smile, and joined her thumb and her index finger together to give me the okay sign. So I kept on going. But something about the woman seemed familiar. I was a few miles down the road when the light came on in my head; it was Kim! I hadn't thought about her in years. What was she doing here? On impulse, I made a U-turn and went back to where the Jag was parked.

Imagine that! A black Mercedes was now parked behind the Jaguar and a man was talking to the damsel in distress inside the green car. I kept my distance and my eyes wide open. Sure enough, Kim got out of the Jaguar and into the Mercedes. They drove off. I thought about going over and slashing the tires of the Jaguar—me, the law abiding middle-aged mother of two. Besides, I bet the Jaguar was either leased or "borrowed" from some poor heartbroken sucker. Fortunately, it was time to meet my clients and that distracted me from thinking about Kim.

I believe life is full of surprises and, once again, I wasn't proven wrong.

I was on one of our monthly home tours, when several real-estate agents get together and "tour" their listings of homes for sale, and we exchange information and input on prices, presentation and such. The last house on tour was a charming cottage in the older part of town. Very small with a lot of character, it had been completely redone without changing its authenticity. It was picture-perfect and yet something was missing. I couldn't tell if someone was living there or if the furnishing, artwork, and accessories were staged. I asked the listing agent.

"Funny you asked," she said. "It's a strange situation, not a happy one. Please don't repeat this because we want good vibes. The owner is a single lady; she bought the house and did the whole refurbishing. It was going to be her love nest. She went way over budget and two weeks before the wedding her fiancé took off with her maid of honor and the last draw the bank released as payment to the contractor. There, that's her portrait, over the fireplace mantel. Poor Kim, she's such a nice person, but now she has a broken heart and an empty wallet."

Kim? That Kim? No, the portrait didn't look like the Kim I remembered; this Kim was nice and plump, with long hair and a motherly smile. Her eyes were blue. Hmm . . . Now I was curious. Once I got back to the office I pulled up the assessor's Web site and checked the address. I'll be! There was her name, date of purchase, and even the price she paid. It was her. Caught at her own game! I wanted to call everyone who ever knew Kim and spread the news, but deep inside I didn't feel too good about it. I called back the agent who had Kim's house listed to see if I could get more inside information. I told her half the truth and asked if Kim was still in town. She said no, Kim wanted a change of scenery; she was hired by a cruise line as an activity director for seniors.

Like I said, life is full of surprises. I wonder what nice story dear Kim was telling her new audience on that luxury liner. Then again, who knows? She may be a changed woman. Oops, I mean, a changed lady.

"If truth is beauty, how come no one has their hair done in a library?"—Lily Tomlin

Five Celebrity Baby Boomer Diehards

These diehards are a very interesting bunch. While they all have many wonderful qualities, a common factor surfaced in all of them: relationship problems.

It appears that regardless of the fact that they'd be married or just "seeing" someone, they are never alone. Almost as if they can't be without a partner, ever. Often the new love interest is already around before the official good-byes are said to the old love interest.

Danielle Steel

Birthday: August 14, 1947

Diehard Qualities: No matter what the critics have said, Steel has continued to write the books she loves and fans worldwide love them, too. She made *Guinness World Records* thanks to her 381 consecutive weeks on the *New York Times* best-seller list. Since her first book was published, every one of her novels has hit best-seller lists in paperback. Steel's novels have been translated into twenty-eight languages and can be found in forty-seven countries worldwide. Twenty-two of her books have been adapted for television, including two that have received Golden Globe nominations. In 2005, Steele reached an agreement with New Line Home Entertainment to sell the film rights to thirty of her novels. New Line is expected to adapt the books as television movies or for the direct-to-video market.

Trivia: Her father was John Schulein Steel, a direct descendant of the founders of Lowenbrau beer. In 2002, Steel, who lives part of the year in France, was decorated by the French government as a "Chevalier" of the Ordre des Arts et des Lettres, for her contributions to world culture.

Cosmetics giant Elizabeth Arden launched a perfume called Danielle by Danielle Steel. The fragrance is a mix made of mandarin, jasmine, orchid, rose, amber, and musk.

Love Life: In 1965, when she was only eighteen, Steel married banker Claude-Eric Lazard. After nine years of marriage, Steel's relationship with Lazard ended.

Steel married again, but at the time of the ceremony, the groom, Danny Zugelder, was in jail. The marriage ended quickly, and Zugelder was later convicted of a series of rapes.

Steel married her third husband, heroin-addicted William Toth, the day after her divorce from Zugelder was final. She was eight and a half months pregnant with Toth's child. This marriage ended within two years.

But Steel was still optimistic about finding love. She married for the fourth time in 1981, to vintner John Traina. After her divorce from Traina, Steele married for a fifth time, to Silicon Valley financier Tom Perkins, but the marriage lasted less than two years, ending in 1999.

Danielle married and divorced five times. She is single now, but who knows for how long?

Stevie Nicks

Birthday: May 26, 1948

Diehard Qualities: Stephanie Lynn Nicks has been through two major addictions: drugs and Lindsey Buckingham. Although she had achieved significant critical acclaim, by 1985 drugs were taking a toll on her performing by severely limiting her vocal range and pitch. The drugs also affected her onstage persona. At the end of Fleetwood Mac's Australian tour, Nicks checked herself into the Betty Ford Center to treat her cocaine addiction. In 1993 Nicks tripped and gashed her forehead on a fireplace but didn't even feel any pain. She realized she needed help and endured a painful forty-seven-day detox from Klonopin in the hospital.

After she completed treatment for her addictions, she vowed never to publicly perform again. But she came out of retirement to perform on Fleetwood Mac's 1997 reunion tour. She continues to write, record, and perform.

Trivia: As a member of Fleetwood Mac, she was inducted into the Rock and Roll Hall of Fame in 1998. Stevie has a brother named Christopher who is married to Lori Perry, one of Stevie's backup singers and the ex-wife of producer Gordon Perry. Accolades continued when *People* magazine named Nicks one of the 50 Most Beautiful People. Nicks owns a strand of Janis Joplin's stage beads.

Love Life: Nicks first met her future musical and romantic partner Lindsey Buckingham during her senior year at Menlo Atherton High School. She and Buckingham attended a religious meeting, where together they sang "California Dreamin'." Buckingham remembered Nicks's enchantingly unique voice and a few years later, he contacted Nicks and asked her to join a band called Fritz, which became a popular live act from 1968 until 1972. To keep the pair financially afloat, Nicks worked a variety of jobs, which included waiting tables and a stint cleaning engineer/producer Keith Olsen's house while Buckingham, who was recovering from mono, lived there, writing music and practicing guitar.

Their debut album, *Buckingham Nicks,* caught the attention of drummer Mick Fleetwood of Fleetwood Mac. Initially, Fleetwood was interested only in Buckingham, but Buckingham said that he would only join if Nicks was also invited into the group, stating firmly that he and Nicks were a "package deal." The duo joined Fleetwood Mac on December 31, 1974.

The great love affair had major ups and down during the recording of their album *Rumors* in 1976. Nicks's contributions were the jaunty, "I Don't Want to Know" (intended for a second Buckingham/Nicks album in 1974); the dark, mystical "Gold Dust Woman," a diatribe about the dangers of cocaine and the rock and roll lifestyle; the dramatic "Silver Springs," a b-side about her relationship with Buckingham. The ensuing tour was another great success for the band, during which time they all began relationships outside the group.

Playing up to the media image of Fleetwood Mac as two sparring, romantically entangled couples, *Mirage* was released in June 1982 with a cover photo featuring Nicks in the arms of Lindsey Buckingham. Although Nicks and Buckingham have gone their separate ways and Lindsey is married with children, the old sexual tension is ever present when they perform together.

Christie Brinkley

Birthday: February 2, 1954

Diehard Qualities: In 1976, Christie signed a contract with cosmetics giant CoverGirl, which they continued to renew for twenty years. In 2005, a few years after CoverGirl ended their contract with Brinkley, they again signed her on as a model. She has appeared in many magazines and commercials for mature skin products since then. She appeared on the cover of three consecutive *Sports Illustrated* swimsuit issues (1979–1981), and was also in their fortieth anniversary hall of fame issue.

Brinkley has been with the Ford Modeling Agency for over thirty years. She is an accomplished photographer, designer, artist, and fitness expert. And she has been married four times.

Trivia: As a child, Christie used to own an English sheepdog named Shakespeare.

She speaks French fluently.

Brinkley was Don King's ring photographer for major boxing events.

She is a supporter of animal rights and a long-time PETA member.

Love Life: Brinkley's first marriage (1973–1981) was to Jean-François Allaux, an artist and illustrator she met in France. She then dated Oliver Chandon de Brailles, heir to the Moët-Chandon champagne fortune. Chandon died in an auto-racing accident in 1983.

Two years later she married musician Billy Joel and went on to inspire his hit "Uptown Girl" and several other songs. In 1994 the couple divorced, and Brinkley married Richard Taubman. Those two split less than a year later, supposedly after Taubman failed to repay a $1.5 million loan.

Her fourth husband is Peter Cook, an architect she married in 1996. Brinkley filed for divorce from Cook in the summer of 2006 after news spread that he had an alleged extramarital affair with a nineteen-year-old.

Just think about her disastrous love life. With the exception of Billy Joel, all her other husbands or love interests let her down. Well, Christie is still smiling and looking like a million-dollar baby. This Uptown Girl has real class, a lot of love to share, and possibly an eye out for husband #5.

Chris Evert

Birthday: December 21, 1954

Diehard Qualities: Evert won at least one Grand Slam singles title each year for thirteen consecutive years from 1974 through 1986. She never lost in the first round of a Grand Slam singles tournament, her earliest exits being in the third round. Evert won the French Open singles title a record seven times. She was ranked number one in the world for five consecutive years between 1974 and 1978. When she first started playing tennis as a youngster, she developed a two-handed backhand because she was too small and weak to hit backhand shots with one hand. This became a trademark of her game and inspired generations of future players.

Trivia: Evert's career win-loss record in singles matches of 1,309-146 (.900) is the best of any professional player in tennis history. She was also considered the women's tour leader in dirty jokes. Evert hosted the TV show *Saturday Night Live* on November 11, 1989. She was the first tennis player and only female tennis player to host the show as of its airing.

Love Life: Evert's romance with the top men's player Jimmy Connors captured the public's imagination in the 1970s, particularly after they both claimed the singles titles at Wimbledon in 1974. They became engaged, but the romance did not last. A wedding planned for November 8, 1974, was called off. But her love affair with athletes continued.

In the years that followed, Evert was romantically linked with several other high-profile men. She reportedly had affairs with, among others, Vitas Gerulaitis and John Gardner.

In 1979, Evert married British tennis player John Lloyd. This marriage ended in divorce in 1987. In 1988, Evert married two-time Olympic downhill skier Andy Mill. They have three sons—Alexander James (born 1991), Nicholas Joseph (born 1994), and Colton Jack (born 1996). On November 13, 2006, Evert filed for divorce. The divorce was finalized on December 4, 2006, with Evert rumored to have paid Mill a settlement of $7 million in cash and securities. She and Australian golfer Greg Norman announced in September 2007 their intention to marry. They were together at her annual charity event in Boca Raton in November 2007. Will he finally be the athlete for her?

Sharon Stone

Birthday: March 10, 1958

Diehard Qualities: After a series of minor movies, Stone's appearance in *Total Recall* with Arnold Schwarzenegger gave her career a welcome jolt. To coincide with the movie's release, she posed nude for *Playboy* magazine, showing off the buff body she developed in preparation for the movie. She later stated that she posed for the magazine because she needed the money. In 1999, Stone was rated among the twenty-five sexiest stars of the century by *Playboy*.

The role of Catherine Tramell, a cocaine-snorting, bisexual, mind-game-playing serial killer in the movie *Basic Instinct* finally brought Stone international acclaim. In the movie's most notorious scene, Tramell is being questioned by the police and she crosses and uncrosses her legs revealing the fact she was not wearing any underwear. To this day, Stone claims to have been tricked into the stunt. The movie became the number-one box-office hit of the year. That same year, she was rated by *People* magazine as one of the fifty most beautiful people in the world.

Basic Instinct 2: Risk Addiction was released on March 31, 2006. By Sunday, April 2, 2006, after earning $3.2 million in its debut weekend, the movie was declared a bomb. Here is where her true diehard instinct shows best. *Basic Instinct 2* didn't turn out too well? Even so, Sharon Stone has said she would love to do a *Basic Instinct 3*.

Trivia: In the early 1990s, Stone became a member of the Church of Scientology. She is also an ordained minister with the Universal Life Church.

Not long after the release of *Total Recall*, Stone was involved in a car accident on Sunset Boulevard in Los Angeles. The accident left her with scars that are visible in some of her later screen appearances.

Stone's first taste of show business was with the Ford Modeling Agency in New York. Stone spent a few years modeling, and appeared in TV commercials for Burger King, Clairol, and Maybelline.

In March 2007, Stone returned to Edinboro University, where she once was a student and, there, to her surprise, she received an honorary doctorate from the University president.

Stone lives in Beverly Hills, California, and also owns a ranch in New Zealand. In March 2006, Stone traveled to Israel to promote peace in the Middle East through a press conference with Nobel Peace Prize winner Shimon Peres.

Love Life: Sharon Stone was married and divorced three times. She's now single.

Want more prove of her impulsive-repetitive nature? While married to her third husband, they adopted a boy named Roan Joseph, born in 2000. And then, on May 2005, Stone adopted a baby boy who had been born in Texas to a surrogate mother. She named the baby boy Laird Vonne Stone. In June 2006 Stone adopted another baby boy named Quinn. In August 2006, Stone confirmed that she adopted another baby boy. That's three babies in twelve months and four altogether! Angelina who?

The Ultimate Quiz

The Ultimate Quiz

No book on love would be complete without a quiz, so here it is. This quiz is about you and what you'll do for love. Take a seat, grab a pen, and stroll down the magical avenue of What If.

1. You've received an announcement for your high school reunion in the mail. You:

   a. Decide to move to New Guinea; you understand mail travels slow there.

   b. Can't decide whether you'll go. Could you pimp a ride there and back?

   c. Immediately call your plastic surgeon, the beauty salon, and Weight Watchers.

   d. Wonder if that geek you had a crush on will be there. More important, would he remember you?

   e. Think, "Great, I'll have a chance to catch up with old friends."

2. You no longer live in the same state where you went to high school so you think to yourself:

   a. Like I'm going to blow my money to go see some losers?

   b. Time to call in some past-due favors and get a free bed, breakfast, and, who knows, a little sex?

   c. Whoa, if I work out a little harder I can wear that new sexy outfit.

    d. I need to find out what the weather is like there; I may want to splurge on a new coat.

    e. If I do go, do I need to reserve a room at a local hotel? How about room sharing?

3. As the reunion day approaches, you ask yourself:

    a. Can you imagine that? They want the money in advance?

    b. Maybe I can borrow my friend's evening gown?

    c. Is this the perfect time to try that hairdo I've always dreamed of?

    d. Should I send a check or use a charge card?

    e. Should I offer to help with the planning?

4. You've paid the fees and committed to go, now you say to yourself:

    a. What was I thinking? Can I rent a date?

    b. Okay, maybe I can buy a new outfit, leave the tags on, and then return it.

    c. I love my new hairdo. I think it makes me look ten years younger.

    d. Gee, what if there is a storm and the plane can't take off?

    e. I'll make copies of our last class photo and bring one for everybody.

5. One week to go and counting:

    a. Okay, okay, don't panic. I can always back out at the last minute.

b. There is no way I'll get away with this. How about a corsage to hide the tags?

c. I think I'll have some fake eyelashes put on; they look so good on the "Desperate Housewives."

d. To whom did I lend my suitcase? Or was I the one borrowing it?

e. Whoever invented high school reunions deserves a monument.

6. The big day is here. You sign in and get your name tag while musing:

a. What nerve, how can they not remember my name?

b. I'm glad I'm here, even if it did cost way too much.

c. Everybody is looking at me; you think they know I'm wearing silicon bust enhancers?

d. What's for dinner, and whom can I sit with?

e. See how great we all look? And so many of us are single again!

7. The party is over and it's time to say good-bye. You:

a. Swear this is the last high school reunion you'll ever go to.

b. Make sure you have all your receipts for taxes—you *did* talk business after all.

c. Maybe I shouldn't have gotten so tipsy and sung "Memories" to my classmates.

d. What do you know, the former geek is a dot-com magnate, *and* he remembered me. *And* we exchanged phone numbers.

e. What a wonderful group of people, and how some have blossomed. I was hoping to rekindle an old flame. Oh well, maybe next time.

Here is how you score the quiz:

Every A answer is 0 points
Every B answer is 1 point
Every C answer is 2 points
Every D answer is 3 points
Every E answer is 4 points

If you scored between 20 and 28, you are whatever you want to be: trailblazer, lover, diehard. Perhaps you tend to grow tired of the same interaction and you need constant excitement to keep you interested. Because you are a great mix of the three categories, you are able to attract a variety of lovers. The problem is you seem to always search for more. This could be due to your quest for the perfect, yet elusive relationship: think soul mate or just plain boredom. Father Time hasn't slowed you down. Could true love do?

If you scored between 13 and 20, you are definitely a trailblazer. You also have what it takes to make a good lover. The question is, do you want to? It seems as though you are so used to creating your own entertainment that you don't always yearn for companionship.

If you scored between 9 and 13, you are in touch with your body and your needs. You are indeed a diehard by nature and you are ready not only to love but most important, give love. You'll never be lonely or alone; love is with you when you are up and when you are down. You spread hope and goodwill.

If you scored between 6 and 9, you are a combination of lover and trailblazer. Both traits are equally balanced. Problem is, you are not comfortable with the combination, and you feel compelled to be one or the other. My question to you is why? Relax and believe me. In this case, more is better.

If you scored 5 or less, you are a lover in disguise. Sure you put up a great front. That's in self-defense. You've been hurt and you don't want to see that happen again. Underneath all that acting, there is a nurturing soul ready to blossom. Go ahead, let it be, the world could always use more love.

Trivia:
The Common
Factor

Trivia:
The Common Factor

Guess what these boomers have in common:

Kim Bassinger
Dennis Rodman   **They all posed in the nude for**
The Go-Gos   **the** *"I'd rather go naked than wear fur"*
Melissa Etheridge   **PETA campaign.**

Roger Moore   Besides the fact that they are English
Pierce Brosnan   and handsome?
Timothy Dalton   **They all played agent 007 James**
                       Bond in the movies.

Natalie Vadim
Portia Rebecca   **They are all related to Jane**
    Crockett   **Fonda.**
Bridget Fonda
Christian Vadim

Cher
Meg Ryan
Heather Locklear   **They all have tattoos.**
Tommy Lee

Amanda Root
Colin Firth
Emma Thompson   **They all appeared in screen ver-**
Peter Firth   **sions of Jane Austen's novels.**
Fiona Shaw

One More for the Road

One More for the Road
In their own words.

One last real-life romance, "for inspiration," as Madonna would say.

Q: Hi, Gordon and Deni. You two met online, or so the story goes?

Gordon: We were both members of an online writers' group, and our paths did cross, occasionally, and fiery words did fly through the ether between Australia and Colorado, yes.

Deni: Gordon had published twenty Harlequin romances as Victoria Gordon and would sign his posts Gordon/Victoria. One day he sent me a personal message and signed it "El Gordo." I didn't know who the heck he was, but his words were . . . fiery . . . so I had to respond.

Q: Fiery words, but no romantic sparks?

Gordon: Not for a few years. Then that woman had the temerity to suggest we ought to try and write a book together. I, of course, scoffed at such nonsense. But she got her way—girls usually do.

Deni: Since I was writing mysteries and Gordon was writing romances, I suggested we write a romantic suspense together. Of course, I had to change all his "girls" to "women."

Q: And you did write the book together?

Gordon: Oh, we did indeed. It's called *Finding Bess*—her idea of a title (or maybe mine . . . I forget). Indeed we wrote the entire book online, half a world apart and still without having actually met. It was an . . . interesting exercise.

Deni: Gordon came up with the title. My job was to "Americanize" the American heroine. Soon I found myself using expressions like "Bloody oath!" in ordinary conversation. My friends thought I was bonkers.

Q: More than that, surely. Didn't you become "involved" while writing it?

Gordon: Well, that's Deni's story. You must ask her. She'll give you a lot of nonsense answers, of course, but the truth of it is that I simply seduced her via the Internet. I am a romance writer, after all. But it was a lot of work, let me tell you. The poor girl could only spell in American, while I am fluent in Canadian, British, Australian, and American. And she'd never been out of the continental U.S. in her life and the book was set in Australia. There were . . . problems.

Deni: I kept telling him I didn't want to get romantically involved, but the man wooed me. With words. Naturally, there were . . . problems.

Q: Such as . . . ?

Gordon: Well, she's a mystery author, for starters. And they're a weird mob at the best of times and worse when in the throes of being seduced. I kept trying to spice up the romantic elements of our book and she kept trying to insert clues and red herrings. And we'd never physically met, which rather complicated everything.

Deni: Gordon wanted to meet, in person. I had a deadline for a novella. I couldn't just hop a plane for Australia.

Q: So where and when did you actually meet?

Gordon: On a cold, sunny day in June, at the airport in Launceston, Tasmania.

Deni: I hopped a plane for Australia.

Q: And did you fly into each other's arms in true romantic fashion?

Gordon: Yes, once I'd figured out who she was—she'd only ever sent me baby photos during our courtship. Typical feminine cunning.

Deni: Yes, we flew into each other's arms. I had sent him my latest dust-jacket portrait, along with some pictures from my childhood. Plus, a candid photo of me in shorts. He framed that picture because (in Gordon-speak) I was "wearing legs."

Q: And now you're married and living in Canada? Why Canada?

Gordon: Australia was too remote, from many points of view. And I have family here . . . I started out Canadian, after all. It seemed like a good compromise. So after Deni's Australian visit, we both sold up and moved here to Vancouver Island. Then we ferried over to Vancouver for the Novelists Inc. writers conference—the organization through which we met—and got married during the conference, which seemed appropriate.

Deni: I loved Australia, but my career is North American–based. We mutually agreed to buy a house in British Columbia.

Q: So what's it like, having two published authors living in the same house?

Gordon: It's hell, pure unadulterated hell. There is this phenomenon called "cabin fever," which is very common in remote areas. People live too close and get on each other's nerves. Not a problem for us, of course, because I hardly ever see Deni. In fact, I'm sure I actually "talked" to her more when I was in Australia. Nowadays, she rises early, removes her illustrious presence to her office, and I'm lucky if I see her for the rest of the day.

Deni: It's heaven, glorious heaven. Gordon and I don't always have the same tastes when it comes to food, movies, or art, but he understands that an author can become obsessed with a work in progress. Gordon knows better than to interrupt me at play . . . I mean, work.

Q: You have separate offices, then?

Gordon: Oh yes. We hadn't been in the house a week and I was busy building her this Taj Mahal of an office. She gets the fax machine and photocopier, and the one heating vent (I get to fetch the firewood) and she's closer to the kitchen and the loo.

Q: But you both get work done?

Gordon: Writing, you mean? Well, *she* certainly does. The woman's extremely professional, works very hard. Misses lunch regularly (in the throes of creativity, you understand). Sometimes she even misses dinner.

Deni: We've gotten a ton of work done. Gordon has even written three screenplays and a stage play.

Q: Do I detect a note of bitterness from you, Gordon?

Gordon: Bitter? Me? Would you call a man bitter just because he whines at having to send his wife e-mails from upstairs to downstairs if he wants any sort of conversation during office hours?

Q: You actually send each other e-mails . . . within the same house?

Gordon: Better than shouting. No woman enjoys being shouted at, eh? And neither of us enjoys being disturbed while working, so it's a sort of compromise. Deni's done a power of work since she came to Canada; we both have. And it couldn't have gotten done if we didn't take a reasonably professional attitude about our writing.

Deni: Gordon sends me lovely e-mails. He's so romantic. I have to say, you've never been romanced until you've been romanced by a romance author.

Q: What, exactly, have you accomplished since you got together? Writing-wise, that is?

Gordon: Well, in between fetching firewood, mowing lawns, carpentering, painting, fencing, building offices, minding the dog, etc., I wrote three screenplays, reworked the novel on which I based the first screenplay, finished off a variety of projects including my feral-cat novel *Cat Tracks*, wrote a crime fiction novel called *The Specialist*, then wrote the sequel, *Dining with Devils*. I also carved an eight-foot cedar stump on my front boulevard, and, well, heaps of stuff.

Deni: I've written heaps of stuff. Most recent, *Chain a Lamb Chop to the Bed*, the third book in my Ellie Bernstein/Lt. Peter Miller "diet club" series and *The Landlord's Black-eyed Daughter* under a new pen name, Mary Ellen Dennis.

Q: Do you think you would have "connected" had you not met online?

Gordon: No. The distance was too great.

Deni: Of course we would have met. Gordon is my soul mate.

Q (laughing): Who's the "romantic" now?

Dean Stevenson, Stevenson's Studio LLC

Maria Grazia Swan is a writer and Realtor based in Phoenix, Arizona. When her house was burned down by a stalker in 1998, she became an advocate for the safety of people living alone. As a result, she began getting more single clients in her real-estate business. Soon after that, she started hosting singles parties and is now responsible for bringing together a number of happy couples.

Swan is a columnist for the online magazine *Single for Now* and gives relationship advice on the website RealEstate4Singles. She has also written a monthly column for singles in *Valley Magazine*, based in Orange County, CA. She has been featured several times in the *Arizona Republic* and is the winner of an award from the Women's National Book Association.

Swan emigrated to the United States from Italy in 1969. She is the divorced mother of two and grandmother of two.